'*You are a Mainw[...]*
endowed with ple[...]
bornness of twenty [...]
daughter as she em[...]
Miss Nightingale's [...]

Lady Eustacia Mainwaring, acclaimed beauty and heiress, had amazed London Society by declaring her intention of becoming a common nurse. Now, facing the horrors of war at Scutari, she will need every ounce of her strength and courage. But how could she have remained in comfort in England after reading in the Casualty lists that the only man she will every marry, surgeon Roger Verrall, is 'missing believed killed'?

DESTINY
AT BALACLAVA

ALANNA WILSON

MILLS & BOON LIMITED
London · Sydney · Toronto

First published in Great Britain 1984
by Mills & Boon Limited, 15–16 Brook's Mews,
London W1A 1DR

ISBN 0 263 74668 2

Set in 11 on 12½ pt Linotron Times
04–0584–52,350

Photoset by Rowland Phototypesetting Ltd
Bury St Edmunds, Suffolk
Made and printed in Great Britain by
Cox & Wyman Ltd, Reading

PROLOGUE

IT HAD been a warm and sunny day, drifting hazily into a warm and drowsy evening.

The fifteen ministers of the British Crown had dined well and wined even better. They settled into their comfortable armchairs. Outside the tall windows, pleasant golden light was filtering through green leaves. The ministers relaxed . . . One or two of them stifled yawns.

The voice of the Duke of Newcastle droned on.

'. . . an attack—from which important consequences are anticipated—can no longer be delayed . . .'

Alert to support the words of his colleague, Lord Palmerston sat watching the faces of the others—ready to refute any dissenting voices.

There was none. His intervention, Lord Palmerston realised, would not be necessary. Heads nodded here and there. Perhaps they approved of the Duke's words; or perhaps they dozed . . .

'. . . an early decision to undertake these operations . . .'

The monotonous voice, the warm room, were soporific. Someone made a murmurous sound. Possibly he agreed—or possibly he yawned.

It was 29th June 1854.

Certain of the Cabinet were rather surprised, later, to learn that they had agreed to extend the

Crimean campaign. They did not know how many enemy troops were there; they could not locate the Crimean Peninsula on a map; they did not know what weather would prevail . . . and they sent the British army to an unknown place without provision for correct medical care. (It was cheaper to run a war that way.)

The British public were soon to be surprised also by the reports which began to appear in the morning papers propped against their breakfast marmalade.

'*No preparation for the commonest surgical operations!*' thundered *The Times*. 'Men lie for a week without a medical man coming near—! Men are being left to *die in agony*!'

Faced with these accusations, the army blustered. Such shocking distortions of the truth must be suppressed—they were subversive— they helped the enemy!

The war correspondents, however, continued to write; the dispatches continued to come home to England and be read. Public indignation was fired. It grew, and spread, and swelled into an uproar.

Something had to be done to appease the public anger, and Sidney Herbert, England's Secretary at War, casting about in his mind for someone who possibly could do something about it, thought—with profound relief—of a lady, a Miss Florence Nightingale.

And so it began.

CHAPTER
ONE

EUSTACIA MAINWARING came to Scutari in the
late afternoon. The red windy west was low at
her back. The Turkish caique that carried the
band of women across the sweet waters of the
Bosphorus danced lightly, airily, over the waves.
The air was cold, but the sunlight of the golden
winter day lay like a benison on the pleasant
turf-covered slopes of Constantinople, warming
the travellers as they left the city behind, gilding
the pretty wooden houses nestling in their
vineyards and gardens on the cliffs that faced the
sea.

The faces of Eustacia and her companions
were turned to the eastern horizon, away from
the radiant sky, but the lingering beam of the sun
rested on their backs. It touched the faces of the
Turkish oarsmen and lighted the dark features
with a transient copper glow. One of the women
seated in the caique gave a sigh, and pressed
a narrow hand to the cross that hung upon
her breast. Under the stiff white wimple that
banded her forehead, her eyes were distant,
visionary.

'Ah . . . When we land—let us go straight to nursing the poor fellows.'

The erect stiff figure in the bows did not move or turn her head. Her gaze was fixed on the horizon. Her clipped response, when it came, was uttered in a tone that dismissed any pretensions to noble aspirations or exalted emotions. Her words cast a silence over the rest of the women in the boat.

'The strongest,' said Miss Nightingale tersely, 'will be needed at the wash-tubs.'

Flames of red and gold shot from the dying sun almost to the zenith. The oars flashed in rhythm. As they went, the waters before them broke into flurries of gilded ripples, the wavelets in their wake swirled together, merged, and danced in the light with little curling edges of melted gold.

Towards the rear of the caique, straight-backed upon the narrow bench, Eustacia sat. She sat calmly, gloved hands in her lap, stout black boots planted on the leather portmanteau under her feet. A close grey bonnet covered her tightly plaited hair, but a finger of sunlight sought out the golden strands scraped back from her forehead and slid lovingly over the delicate pure contours of cheekbone, mouth and jaw. The eyes under her slim dark brows were deeply and brilliantly blue, the lashes heavy and black; her chiselled face was pale, but touched beneath the skin by the warmth of youth and health. Under its drab covering of grey dress and grey cloak, her slim long-legged body was taut and strong and supple.

A broadside slap set the boat shuddering. Eustacia braced herself on the hard seat and gazed ahead, past the bonnets and shoulders of those in front, outlined now against the paling sky. Her eyes reached and searched beyond the boatrail and onwards to the point which marked the meeting of sea and sky. A raw wind gusted into her face as the sun died; she raised her chin against it, and drew the grey cloak closer . . .

It was nine days ago that she had stood with the others upon the deck of the *Vectis* berthed at Marseilles, due out for Constantinople on the evening tide. Some of the women had been accompanied as far as Marseilles by relatives or friends, come to see them safely embarked and to bid them farewell; others stood alone at the rail, or in little groups of two or three, chatting quietly together and watching the activity of the busy dockside below. Forty nurses and nuns, banded and gathered together, and bound for a destination where no female nurse had been before—the Selimeyah Barrack, erstwhile the property of the Turkish army, now a British military hospital at Scutari, focal point for the care of the wounded on the Crimean Peninsula, and three hundred miles across the sea from Balaclava Bay.

Amid the shouting and movement, the last-minute exchanges of tears, kisses and handclasps, Eustacia and her father stood side by side, a little apart. The afternoon was waning, and the air was cold. The Earl bent his handsome head, and quietly took his daughter's hand.

'Tess—even now—it is not too late . . . Are you sure—quite sure—that you wish to do this?'

Eustacia looked up into his eyes. They were blue as her own, and very intent. She saw the faces of the others back in London, trying to smile, waving from the porch steps as she drove away in the carriage with Papa. Her mother, she knew, would go into the house and weep again. She heard the voice of her sister Lucy, incredulous, coaxing, pleading . . . Tess, you cannot do this, you must not, I won't bear it! How can I be happy, with you so far away in that dreadful place—it isn't fair! Then Lucy, too, had cried . . . Remembering, Eustacia's eyes began to cloud and blur; she looked mistily at her father, and said in a shaky whisper,

'Papa—dear Papa! To cause you all so much pain . . . I am truly sorry for it.'

Her tears spilled over.

The Earl extracted a large white handkerchief from his pocket and carefully dried his daughter's eyes. She gulped and swallowed, and went on more steadily, 'If I could only feel that you understood—'

Lord Cumnor pinched her chin.

'I understand this much,' he said wryly. 'You are a Mainwaring, my girl, and therefore endowed with plenty of courage, and the stubbornness of twenty devils.' Eustacia's lips trembled, she smiled up at him through her tears. Her father put an arm about her and drew her close against him. 'Go with my blessing, love! Only take care. We want to see you safe back again.' He was silent for a moment. His arm tightened and he said again, very low, 'Take care, my Tess.'

'I shall,' she choked. She threw her arms around him; they exchanged a last heartfelt hug. Then the Earl released her, and turned quickly away.

Eustacia's eyes followed his tall figure as he descended the gangway, and searched for him among the crowded figures on the dock. The plank was hoisted; the ship began to vibrate, to move. The girl strained her eyes through the gloom of the afternoon. The *Vectis* drew away from the wharf—the gap of water widened. They set sail for the open sea . . .

The elbow of the nurse beside her in the caique nudged Eustacia briskly in the ribs.

'Look! There it is!'

Eustacia gave a little start, and focused her eyes on the immediate present. Staring before them, the band of women watched as the vast black bulk of the Selimeyah Barrack rose up from the darkening shoreline. The caique carried them closer and they began to discern, at angles of the sprawling structure, square towers that pointed upwards to a heaven now tinted with opal and pearl. There were other buildings flanking the Barrack, clustering or spreading on either side, but it overshadowed them all.

Eustacia stared, with slightly parted lips; beside her, the other nurse fell silent.

Gradually the caique drew near to the shore. A murmur of anticipation ran through the company of women. The shape of a wooden jetty emerged from the dusk before them.

A sudden sharp wind blew in their faces. It was heavy; redolent of something that had nothing to do with the clean salty air. A stronger gust came to them, bringing a smell that curled round their nostrils. At the boatrail, one of the nurses looked down and quietly drew the edge of her cloak across her mouth.

The caique had slowed, and began nosing its way through a sea which had become strangely sluggish and oily. The prow bumped gently against unseen obstructions that momentarily impeded it, and then slid away, glistening in the slanting light. A scum lay on top of the water. It heaved with the sea-swell, slowly, and gurgled at the edges, leaving curves of slimy deposits upon the black churned-up mud.

The caique grated against the jerry. The boatmen shipped their oars.

Eustacia picked up her portmanteau. One by one the nurses clambered to the landing-stage; the line of grey figures, luggage in their hands, set off in double file along the jetty. The waters that sucked around the wooden pylons beneath their feet were full of debris. Refuse, of a sort that defied description, hung just below the surface, heaved dully into sight, rolled under again. From below the jetty, as they walked above, a cloud of flies rose up. Down there in the mud a dead horse lay, stiff-legged and distended; a gaunt dog tore at the carcass with yellow fangs. The silent procession passed by, wending its way to the end of the landing-place, and the disturbed flies buzzed and flew, and settled to their work again.

As the nurses approached the looming Barrack, they found that the front entrance of the place was enclosed by a courtyard. The door was opened to them after a little wait; they passed inside and stood within the courtyard, looking up at the façade that towered above and stretched away on each side. The courtyard was wet with a sort of slime that was liquid and had slipped into little black runnels between the stones and collected in oleaginous pools in the uneven places. The stench that arose from this wrapped itself around them, catching at throats and corroding the nostrils; it was almost vaporous, almost a visible miasma, foetid and clinging. A nurse made a tiny choking sound which turned into a cough.

The heavy front door swung open at last. The cloaked figures entered the building.

Eustacia followed at the rear as the group made their way along a dark passage lit by a Turkish lamp in the hand of their guide. They stopped in front of a closed door. A muffled conversation took place, but Eustacia, at the back of the phalanx, could not hear what was said. The door was opened; the lamp held high; they filed into the room.

It was a dim and draughty apartment faintly lit by a couple of oil lamps, and the cold of it struck into the bone; the air had the dank-edged bite of the vault. The room contained a row of cross-legged cots, bare of any coverings except for straw pallets. As far as could be distinguished in the crowding shadows there was nothing else in the room by way of furnishings. The old wooden floorboards were sodden, and beads of moisture oozed and glistened in clammy trickles down the walls.

One or two of the women whispered; but for the most part they waited quietly, with still eyes, and faces turned towards their leader.

Eustacia was standing just inside the entrance. The rays of the lamp were feeble; they flickered in the draught. Parts of the room were not illuminated. In the wavering light, Eustacia glanced about and became gradually aware of a truckle-bed placed apart from the others, almost behind the door, and half hidden in shadow. She looked more closely; her sharp eyes made out something more than the bare outline of the mattress. She took a step towards it, and another.

A man was stretched upon the cot. He lay upon his back. Eustacia peered, and drew close. Leaning over him, she saw that he wore the long grey coat of a Russian soldier, and that his uniform bore the insignia of the Tsarist Imperial Army.

She looked into his face; it was the most nearly colourless that she had ever seen on a human being. The features were blanched, drained to the whiteness of bone. His lower jaw was hanging loose, disclosing white teeth in bone-white gums; even his fair hair seemed bleached by death. The skirts of the greatcoat were saturated, dark with a stain that had spread to the naked straw beneath him and dripped through the wooden slats of the bed to the dirty floor.

Despite the bulky covering of the heavy coat, it was plain to see that his legs were gone.

Eustacia gave a long involuntary shudder, born of horror and of pity. She stiffened her body and set her teeth, but for a moment the blue-white face quivered in a macabre jig before her eyes. She uttered a tiny gasp, and stretched out a blind hand to steady herself.

Her hand was taken by another. The nurse who had travelled next to her in the caique had come up beside her in the gloom.

Eustacia breathed, 'His legs . . .'

They looked together, for a minute. The other

girl whispered, 'Such loss of blood—he could not have lived.'

Eustacia took a handkerchief from her pocket, unfolded the linen square and laid it over the terrible face. She swallowed once, and spoke calmly.

'Please—would you tell Miss Nightingale? I shall wait here beside him.'

Her companion nodded, and glided away.

They came to the Crimea to ease the maimed, the sick and the dying. It was strange that their first encounter should be with the enemy . . .

That he was Russian made no difference. In a half-circle, the women gathered about him. Rosary beads clicked gently; a nun's voice intoned quietly in the silence of the cold dirty room.

In the weeks that were to come, the nurses of the Barrack Hospital at Scutari would watch over dying that seemed endless.

'I stand,' said Florence Nightingale, 'at the altar of murdered men . . .'

CHAPTER
TWO

'IT'S BEEN days—'

'And days! And still we are not allowed to enter the wards!'

'Disgraceful—'

One of the nurses primmed up her mouth.

'The head surgeon says—'

'I know, I know!' Another voice chimed in, mimicking a fussy and peevish tone. '"Females are not, and never shall be, permitted in military hospitals"!'

There was a burst of angry laughter.

'The head surgeon,' said somebody with a snap, 'should shut up his jaw! How I should like to tell him so!'

A chorus of approval greeted this forthright statement.

At the far end of the room, a lady sat writing at a small wooden table. She lifted her head and glanced towards them; the voices diminished to rebellious whispers.

'We sit here and wait—while the doors are closed in our faces.'

'Why doesn't she insist? I think she should!'

A more reasonable voice interposed.

'She can hardly do that. How can we get into the wards by force?'

There was a pause. The impatient speaker said reluctantly, 'We can't, I suppose. But all the same—'

'It's very hard; all that we can hope for is that he will change his mind.'

'And in the meantime we do nothing!'

The nurses were grouped at one end of their quarters, busily tearing and rolling bandages. The apartment which to date had served them for sleeping, eating and cooking had been scrubbed and scrubbed again. The walls were scoured and the floorboards white. Clean linen—provided by Miss Nightingale—covered the beds. A step past the doorsill took them into squalor, but here, in their own place, they had made a tiny oasis of decent cleanliness and order. It was, so far, all that they had been allowed to do.

Eustacia looked up.

'Here is Mrs Thiele.'

The senior nurse, second in authority only to Miss Nightingale herself, was approaching the group. Mrs Thiele was a spherical lady, tall and imposing, with a handsome strong-boned face and a remarkably level eye. A respectful silence fell as she came towards them, walking with measured yet muted tread between the rows of trestle-beds. One or two of the women straightened their caps.

'Mrs Mainwaring, Mrs Irvine. You may take your exercise now.'

Eustacia and her travelling companion of the caique rose together.

The senior nurse looked them both over with a critical eye. Their plain white caps were set exactly straight upon their braided heads, their grey dresses smooth and neat. Over each girl's shoulders lay a wide white scarf on the back of which were embroidered in red the words, 'Scutari Hospital'. Mrs Thiele studied them, and at last gave a nod.

Moving very quietly past the lady at the desk, Eustacia and the other nurse went to the door. As they quitted the room, Mrs Thiele spoke in a low voice.

'You know the rules. Go only to the eastern tower. Do not speak to any person; do not attempt to look into any of the wards.'

'Yes, Mrs Thiele.'

To reach the eastern tower it was necessary to traverse a very long corridor running almost the sprawling length of the building. Saying no word, with eyes lowered, Eustacia and her companion hastened along this passage. The way was murky, for little natural light filtered in. The two grey-clad figures melted into the gloom and only their white caps and scarves glimmered, like drifting moths, as they moved. At irregular intervals other passages angled away, stretching and vanishing into distant shadows. Doors led off from the corridors here and there, but these were tightly shut.

Outside one of these doors, an orderly lounged at ease, a shoulder propped against the frame. He looked them up and down with a bold grin, and leered at them as they passed. His military tunic was stained and stiff with dirt, and the hand that removed a pipe-stem from his discoloured teeth was black-tipped and grained. As they brushed by him, the smell of spirits came to them. He called some bawdy words after them, with a mocking laugh; they took no notice, but walked calmly on without looking back.

A winding staircase led up into the eastern tower. They reached the foot of it at last, and began climbing to the top with quickening steps.

The room at the top of the tower was small, dusty and empty. Oval-shaped latticed windows were set into the walls, and through these apertures howled a razor-edged wind to chill the heart and marrow. The two nurses, however, were undismayed by this; on the contrary, they catapulted themselves into the room with a rush. Eustacia sped to the nearest window and pressed her forehead to the crisscross slats, taking great gulps of the freezing air, and straining her eyes to peer out over the water.

'Thank heavens!' she gasped, as the raw air caught at her lungs. 'At least we are permitted here—I don't think I could bear it otherwise!'

They had arrived at Scutari in crisp sunny

weather, but this had now given way to dark clammy skies and grey seas wind-driven to racing foam. From their vantage-point high in the tower it was possible to see past the filthy shoreline, to pretend—almost—that it was not there. Far out, on the horizon, white water heaved and tossed. Staring towards it, Eustacia suddenly exclaimed,

'Look, Mrs Irvine! There's a ship out there!'

Faces to the lattice, they peered into the void below and beyond. The wind was blowing hard, sweeping gusts of freezing rain before it, hitting the groaning walls like showers of bullets. The gale was howling dead ashore and, even perched up where they were, the girls could taste the spray salt on their lips. The high waves roared in, shivered and shook, and thundered on the beach; sucking back, they took bites of the muddy edges and left deep hollows behind.

'Can you see the ship still?'

'I've lost it—no, wait! There it is, and another, far out—following behind.'

'Mrs Thiele said that there had been another battle. It must be wounded coming in.'

Eustacia compressed her lips. After a moment, she burst out,

'Wounded coming in! And we can't go near— it's too much!'

'Yes—indeed.'

'We have come all this way—to roll bandages! How stupid men can be!'

'You are right there,' agreed the other.

Eustacia turned her head to her companion. Since their arrival at the hospital there had been little chance for conversation, and even less for the exchanging of confidences. Nevertheless, Eustacia had sensed a warm friendliness in the other girl, and felt drawn towards her. She judged Nurse Irvine to be about twenty, a year or two older than herself. Looking at her now, she saw again, and liked, a pair of dark intelligent eyes, glossy brown hair and a fine clear complexion. Her quick ear had caught a certain soft and musical lilt in Mrs Irvine's voice. Eustacia said, on a note of discovery,

'Ah—now I have it. You are from Wales!'

'I am.' Mrs Irvine smiled. Her mouth was generous, with kindliness and humour about it.

'My name is "Eustacia"—but I'd rather be called "Tess", as I am at home. It still feels strange to me when I am addressed as a married woman, even though I know it is the rule for nurses! But—but I am not married, nor likely to be . . .' She stopped, and turned her eyes away. Presently she said, quietly, 'Please call me "Tess".'

'Thank you . . . I am Rachel.'

'Rachel. And—and are you—?'

'No. I am not married.'

Fierce as it already was, the gale seemed to be growing even more intense. It swept through their eagle's nest, billowing their heavy skirts and thick petticoats. The tower creaked and moaned. Eustacia turned back to the window.

'At home, in the winter, it is like this.'

'Whereabouts is your home?'

'Ribston, in Yorkshire . . .' Tess answered, with faraway eyes. The icy sleet came in from the sea and hissed around the old grey battlements . . . Ribston Castle backed on to the bleak hills, with the stark vista of outcrop and moor beyond, stone towers rising into the freezing sky, dark clouds streaming, the lake whipped up into steely ripples . . . and inside the walls, always, light and warmth and laughter. How lucky we were! Tess thought. No wonder that we vowed, Lucy and I, never to grow up, never to have husbands! She smiled at the memory. She saw pale sunlight on old stone walls, and casements wide in the deep embrasures, birds gliding and dipping over blue waters, and the springtime colours on the moors . . . We said that we would never be married . . . and now Lucy is wed to her only love, and she is happy, as she deserves to be; while I—I shall never be . . .

The grey light filtered through the lattice-work, and found the burnished gold beneath Tess's white cap. Looking at her, Rachel was struck by the untouched beauty of her profile; her face, and her white throat, seemed almost luminous above the drab collar; the deep blue eyes were half-veiled under their heavy fringes. For a brief moment Rachel thought of a church in a green Welsh valley, and of a marble face, sculpted and pure, dimly shining in a shadowed niche high above.

She asked, politely, 'Have you been nursing for very long?'

'When cholera broke out in London I entered the Middlesex Hospital,' Tess replied. 'That was in July. After that, Miss Nightingale agreed to accept me for service here.'

Rachel said in her soft voice, 'I myself began in Germany, in the Protestant hospital.'

'Your parents—did they object?'

'Well . . . My parents are dead—'

'I am sorry.'

'It was long ago . . . I have lived for most of my life with an uncle and aunt.'

'And—did they oppose you?'

'Oh! Very much! My aunt Morgan, in particular. But the Protestant hospital, as you know, is run by women and even the physicians are female; so, under those circumstances, I was able to prevail. But it wasn't easy!'

A responsive flicker chased across Eustacia's face.

'No, indeed. I know just what you mean . . .'

'One does not like to cause distress,' Rachel went on. 'But it is necessary, sometimes, to be firm.' She paused; a smile broke over her face. With amusement in her tone, she added, 'My aunt Morgan cannot be reconciled to it; she is convinced that by becoming a nurse I have permanently lost my reputation. In fact'—with an irrepressible chuckle—'aunt Morgan believes that my only reason for pursuing such an occupation must be that I have fallen in love with some "vulgar, lowborn surgeon"!'

Absolute silence fell in the room. Only the keening voice of the wind curled and whistled, and shook the tower.

Eustacia turned white and cold. It was as if she had been suddenly coated with frost. Her face closed up tight, like a flower touched with ice. She seemed to shrink into her cloak. Before Rachel's appalled gaze, the sapphire eyes turned dark, turned sombre; she withdrew from the girl at her side in a way that was visible and tangible.

'Mrs Mainwaring—Tess!' With stricken eyes, Rachel searched the set profile. 'Forgive me— please! What is it? What have I said?'

There was no answer. Horrified, Rachel watched slow tears escape from under the black lashes and slip down the white cheeks.

Eustacia shook her head, and dashed the tears away with an impatient hand. She swallowed, and spoke through tight lips.

'Good God—what a weakling I am . . . It's nothing. Forget it . . . Please!'

Rachel hesitated, then laid a hand upon her arm.

'You are distressed. I feel that I have caused it . . . If—if you would care to . . . It isn't good, sometimes, to lock things in the heart.'

Eustacia was rigid with suppressed emotion. At last, slowly, she turned her head, and saw the kind eyes close to her own. She bit her lip, removed her gaze back to the sea, and said, on a long sigh,

'I was betrothed to a surgeon . . . Roger Verrall. He—he is missing. I . . . believe him to be dead.'

With instant comprehension, Rachel asked, 'He was here?'

'Yes.'

Rachel said gently, 'What happened?'

'I do not exactly know. He wasn't here at Scutari, you understand. He was across the sea, on the Balaclava side, where the field hospitals are. The surgeons there—go up into the lines . . .'

'I know.'

'And—after the battle at Alma—he was not seen again.'

There was a pause. Rachel said, 'Balaclava is a long way from here.'

'Yes . . .'

'Those hospitals on the other side are out of Miss Nightingale's jurisdiction, as you know; remember, it take two weeks, sometimes, for the wounded to reach Scutari from there. Is it not possible that—Mr Verrall—might have found his way back from the lines, after all, and be there—even now—safe and well?'

'I hope for that, of course . . . but I do not think so.' The white lips stretched into a smile as

Eustacia turned to her friend. 'You mean to comfort me, Rachel, and I am grateful for it. But—but if it had happened so, I am sure that he would, somehow, have contrived to get word to me . . .' She said, with chin lifted, 'We were to be married. Before he sailed from England, he told me that nurses were needed here. That is why I, too . . .' Her words trailed off. She reached into her pocket, and drew out a handsome timepiece, attached by a gold chain to the lining of her cloak. 'We must not stay longer; it's time to go back.'

Without further speech, she left the window and crossed the room. Rachel followed quietly down the twisting stairs.

Lying in the narrow white cot, Eustacia was half-dreaming. She was home in Yorkshire, on a summer morning. The turf bounced underfoot and the early sky was washed in palest blue. She picked up her skirts and ran over the grass; around her, the air was noisy with larksong and the cries of the lapwings.

The cries seemed to be growing louder, more shrill. They broke into her dream and crowded about her. Struggling into wakefulness, she found urgent voices, movement, busy scurryings about her in the dusky room. She looked up into the face of Rachel, who was bending over her, wide-eyed.

'Quickly, quickly! We must hurry!'

Eustacia sat up, and swung her feet to the floor.

'What is it? What's happened?'

'We are sent for! At once! The wounded—there are hundreds! And more ships arriving . . . The surgeons are overwhelmed—'

'We are to go into the wards?'

'Yes! We are needed—'

'At last!'

The door swung open.

'Where should we go?'

'There are orderlies to guide us. Are you ready?'

'Yes! Ready!'

In the wake of the orderly, Eustacia walked into the ward.

The room was long, dim and very crowded. Every bed was full, and men lay on the floor or slumped over against the walls. Above their heads the ceiling was brown and cracked; broken lumps of plaster hung loose, and swayed in the freezing currents of air that swept in through the unglazed windows. Outside the night was dark, with bitter driving rain; it blew into the room and trickled down the walls, forming pools on the filthy floorboards. The air stank—of vomit, gangrene, blood—and it was filled with a low ululation of distress and restless moaning. At the far end, from a bed jammed against the wet wall, a man cried out endlessly; others lay still and grey with the pallor of approaching death; still others twitched and tossed, or crouched doubled up against the walls. Everywhere, under and around the ripped and lacerated bodies, there were dark and spreading stains on the pallets and the floors. Almost at her knee, a blackened swollen face looked up . . . a man with a smashed jaw, holding his arms crossed on his chest as if to contain his unimaginable pain. Another, beside him, seemed unconscious; a fresh sabre-wound ran from his scalp to his throat. The gash had been stitched together, but not bandaged; she bent towards him, and saw moving, threadlike, things in the wound.

Eustacia stood suspended in disbelief.

Beside her appeared a stubbled visage atop a long brown apron that was bloodied from chest to knee.

'Do you know how to set a bone?'

'Yes, sir.'

The surgeon looked doubtfully into her face. Then he nodded, without speaking, and turning on his heel was instantly lost again in the confusion.

It was four o'clock in the morning.

Eustacia had little coherent memory, later, of that dark and bitter day.

On and on, from one to another—rip, cleanse, dress, bind. A boy with glazing eyes looked at her and moved his lips, but no sound came. She touched his face, and murmured, and went on;

there was no time for the hopeless ones when so many were waiting, waiting . . . On and on, forgetting herself, forgetting everything; cutting away at stained filthy clothing, bandaging gaping flesh. She had seen death before, death from cholera, from fever—and it had been ugly and terrible. But this was mutilation of a sort that she had never imagined, of a magnitude to cause a kind of shame, as if intruding upon so huge and awesome a suffering.

She was dazed, her head light, her feet disembodied, but her hands worked on. Now and then she glimpsed other nurses further down the ward; their faces looked stony and expressionless. Her dress was covered in blood and dirt—it caused her no reaction. A curious change began to come over her. It was as though she had become blunted to the fact that this was what war did, and these were the wounded of war, who had been men . . . Her arms and fingers moved mechanically, this one finished, another begun; her heart seemed empty, and her mind dulled. Yet all the time, her lips comforted, her hands touched with gentleness. 'Rest, rest; you will be better soon . . .'

A shaking hand reached up and caught her sleeve. A soldier whispered, 'I am so cold—' He was sitting sideways against the wall, looking up at her. She ripped his tunic open. There was a wound on his chest the size of a small coin. He smiled a little and suddenly fell forward . . .

his back gaped open. He sagged upon her breast, and the rattling breath slowed, and slowed, and died. She laid him down on the wet straw. His face was very pale, but quite unmarked; almost, he could have been asleep and dreaming.

The grey day lightened, and lengthened, and passed again into gloom. She did not know how many hours had gone by. She knelt beside a man whose side and leg were wet with blood, and began to cut away the clothing. He turned dull eyes upon her. His body was pulp from the waist down, flesh and bone were crushed. His blood flowed over her wrist.

Eustacia's stomach gave a desperate heave. She felt an urgent desire to burst out crying. The dripping walls, the dancing lights, the murky room suddenly swam, revolved and receded before her eyes.

'You all right, miss?' The face of the orderly leaning above her was wizened and gap-toothed. His small eyes glinted, his wide mouth was stretched in a friendly grin. 'Cheer up, miss.' With surprising tenderness, he touched her shoulder. 'Worse troubles at sea, they reckon . . . Grindle's the name, miss.'

Eustacia looked up and forced her lips into a pallid smile.

A nun swam noiselessly from the shadows and moved towards them.

'Mrs Mainwaring. You are to rest for an hour.'

Still kneeling, Eustacia gestured towards the dying man.

The nun said with compassion,

'I shall stay with him. Go now, child; Mrs Thiele has ordered it. We shall be working through the night.'

Eustacia rose silently to her feet. As she squeezed past the jammed-in cots, the little orderly whispered,

'You done a good job.'

She nodded slightly, and with lowered eyes left the ward. In the quiet of the nurses' quarters, she lay on her bed and stared at the ceiling.

The days grew darker. The winter deepened into searing blizzards and piercing cold, and the bitter snow fell, mingling with the churned-up mud. Out in the open, the injured lay, in the lines, or on the decks of the hospital ships, exposed to the freezing sleet. The campaign went on. Inkerman was scaled, the heights taken and held, and day and night, without warning, the boats continued to arrive, pouring ever more men into the Barrack hospital. The surgeons worked twenty hours out of the twenty-four; the bay floated with amputated limbs; there was no time for decencies. The men who reached Scutari had already spent a week, perhaps two, lying unattended in the boats on the crossing from Balaclava. They came with wounds, and cholera, and scurvy; encrusted with filth, crawling with lice . . . and still the hospital ships came in and went away like ghosts in the grey rain.

'Two hundred scrubbing-brushes,' wrote the straight-backed lady seated at the wooden table. She moved the lamp a little closer; the flame flickered and dipped. 'Two thousand bars of lye-soap,' ran the neat angular hand. 'Six thousand nightshirts. Six thousand woollen blankets . . .'

CHAPTER
THREE

THE BUILDING rented by Miss Nightingale to serve as the hospital wash-house stood at a little distance from the Barrack. Inside, it was high and spacious, housing rows of tubs set upon wooden benches as well as several huge wash-boilers (procured and paid for by the same lady) in the middle of the room. The boilers gurgled and steamed, fogging the windows with a warm mist. A vast white canopy of drying blankets, sheets and towels hung from clothes-hoists suspended below the ceiling. Soapy bubbles flew from the wash-tubs, and the room was full of the sound of women's voices—good-natured or shrewish—and the shrill echoes of high-pitched laughter.

Children ran about screaming and chirruping, dodging among the tubs and getting underfoot. A burly trooper's wife lifted a moist face from the steaming water and brandished a clothes-stick in their direction; another woman, hefting a basket of dripping linen, narrowly avoided disaster, and sped the unrepentant culprit on his way with a cuff on the ear and an expletive culled from London's East End.

Eustacia and Rachel heaved a soaking blanket from the tub and began to wring the suds from it, twisting and squeezing the heavy folds into a thick rope. A shower of soapsuds scattered in the air. Rachel's cap was crooked, and some tendrils of gold had worked loose from Eustacia's plaits. Grey sleet slashed the windows outside, but within there was moist and pleasant warmth. Both girls were flushed and rather breathless.

Two mischievous urchins darted by, whooping; one cannoned into Eustacia, dived beneath her arm, and went on his way in shrill pursuit of his playmate. Eustacia staggered, and burst out laughing.

'Oh! These children! They are as bad as my brothers!'

'Brothers have I none,' dimpled Rachel. 'How many are you blessed with?'

'Two! Bevan—the younger—is at present in New South Wales, visiting my Aunt Constance. Justin is the eldest of the family . . . Lucy and I bring up the rear!'

'It must be comfortable,' said Rachel, 'to have a brother or two . . .' She added, rather wistfully, 'One's brother would be a special friend, I should think . . .'

'Yes, indeed!' Eustacia agreed, warmly. 'Justin is my most particular friend. He is five years older than Lucy and me, and has always taken care of us—getting us out of scrapes when we were little, and after we grew up . . . even then—' She stopped, abruptly; turned her head away, and appeared to give all her attention to twisting the blanket.

Rachel glanced at her in a little surprise, but said no more.

They doubled the wrung-out rope, and tossed it into a waiting basket.

'It's pleasant here, I think,' Eustacia said. 'The children playing about, and laughing—there is life here.'

'It surprises me,' remarked Rachel, 'to find so many of these women in this place. I would not have expected it, would you?'

'Indeed, no; certainly not two hundred of them,' Eustacia agreed. 'Mrs Thiele was saying that when she went with Miss Nightingale into the basement of the Barrack and discovered them there, most of them were drunk. And, of course, there is cholera among them, too.'

'Yes . . . One can only pity them.'

'That is true! Who can blame them for drinking—finding themselves here, in such conditions! Crammed into that awful basement—I wonder that more of the children have not fallen sick! Why would they come here? It amazes me that they should do so.'

'I think, Tess, that they may have had little choice,' Rachel said shrewdly. 'Follow the drum, or starve; those are their only alternatives, I believe. Here, at least, as soldiers' wives, they are entitled to be fed, and lodged—after a fashion.'

Tess turned wide eyes on her friend.

'I see . . . But what happens, then, to those whose men are killed?'

'I don't know,' Rachel answered, sadly. 'But at least, while they are here, Miss Nightingale has made it possible for them to earn money by working in the wash-house. That must be of some help to them.'

Tess pursed her mouth, thinking.

'Mmm . . . but when they are back in England . . .'

She broke off as a young woman approached between the rows of benches. The newcomer had a pink and pleasant country face, and her dress was clean. She was also heavily pregnant. With a faint sigh, she set down a huge wicker-basket of soiled linen and put a hand to her back.

'Gwen—are you ill?' asked Tess.

'Oh—no, miss, just a twinge.' The girl's round face creased in a smile. 'It's better if I keep on walking about. There's not much ease in lying flat, when you're this far gone!'

'Still, you ought not to carry such heavy loads,' suggested Tess, rather anxiously.

'Bless you—it won't hurt me!' Gwen chuckled, bunching up her red cheeks. 'Why, my Ma had nine of us, miss, and brought up seven—and never missed more'n a day from her work. I'll be just the same, for sure!' The twinkle faded from her eyes, and a cloud passed over her face. 'It's my man that I worry about . . . my Danny. If anything happened to him—'

'He is safe so far, isn't he?'

'Up until three weeks ago, he was safe enough. Johnny Cobb from his regiment told me so.'

'There, then!' Tess exclaimed with warmth. 'He will be fortunate, Gwen—you will see! And you will have a fine son, and all three of you will go home together and live happily ever after!'

Gwen beamed.

'I do hope so, miss!' She picked up the empty basket. 'I'd better be going for another load.' Half-turned away, she hesitated, and added shyly, 'I was wondering—when my time comes—if one of the nurses might be able to—? I'm not afraid—don't think that . . . But it's my first, you see, and—'

Rachel answered kindly, 'One of us will be with you, Gwen. Miss Nightingale is arranging a lying-in room.'

As the girl trod ponderously away, Tess looked after her.

'This is not much of a place—for a child to be born . . .'

*   *   *

The surgeon dipped his hands in the basin of reddened water.

'That's it. You do the leg.' He strode away down the ward.

Tess set down the basin and bent over the cot. The long sabre-cut in the man's chest had been stitched. His legs, however, lay at an angle, broken at the thigh. Tess spoke over her shoulder.

'Grindle. Get the splints, if you please.'

Her hands ran rapidly the length of the injured leg. Quickly and surely, she straightened the bone. 'It's a clean break—he is lucky indeed. Hold the foot, now.'

The small wrinkled face at her shoulder was respectful.

'Better'n a surgeon, you are.' He watched her skilful hands as the long bandage was wound about the splints. 'Wish you'd been around when mine was broke—maybe I wouldn't limp so bad.'

'Never mind,' Tess consoled. 'You are fortunate to have two legs . . . as this man is. I never imagined so many with limbs gone.'

Grindle said chattily, 'Oh! That's the Russki bullets, you see. They smash the bone—and then the gangrene starts—so off it comes! Nothing else for it!'

'I suppose so . . .', Tess sighed, easing the unconscious man back upon the pillow. She listened to his breathing; it was shallow, but regular. Satisfied, she drew the blankets over him.

'Would you take away the screens, Grindle, while I clean up here?'

Grindle obediently removed the heavy screens from around the bed and departed with his burden. Blood had splashed down and stained the clean-scrubbed floor. Tess rolled her sleeves above the elbow and tucked up her skirts. She plunged scrubbing-brush into pail and set vigorously to work. On hands and knees, slim strong arms extended, she slapped the hot soap-suds on the soiled boards. The stain had widened and spread beneath the cot, there was a discoloured patch towards the middle.

She ducked her white-capped head under the bed and reached for the stain with determined brush. Her head and shoulders were hidden and her arms stretched to the fullest. The mark was stubborn; she attacked it grimly.

From somewhere above her, yet close by, a male voice spoke. The voice was cool and languid, and held a faint note of amusement.

'A charming sight!' drawled the disembodied voice. 'Quite charming, by George!'

Tess withdrew her head from beneath the cot. A pair of feet, shod in immaculate boots, was planted on the wet boards. She twisted her neck, and her eyes travelled in surprise along the length of a knife-edged crimson trouser-leg. This was topped by a tunic resplendent with gold lace.

An ornate sabre-tache dangled from a taut waist; she glimpsed a white-gloved hand resting on a hip and, under the black and gold shako of a cavalry officer, a cold high-nosed countenance with curved moustache and supercilious eyebrows.

'A damned pretty sight,' reiterated the newcomer, coolly running an appraising eye over Tess's kneeling figure. 'I didn't expect to find it here; no, indeed, m'dear!'

Two spots of bright red appeared in Tess's cheeks. She turned her head away, and with deliberate care wrung out the floorcloth and mopped up the remaining suds. Then she rose to her feet.

'That's better. Now I can see you properly.' The officer studied her features with lingering eyes and open approval. 'Why! A beauty, no less! And as for the angle from which I first observed—' his mouth curled, under the black moustache—'entirely pleasing! I assure you!'

He stood squarely in her path, making no move to allow her to pass in the narrow space between the cots. Keeping his eyes fixed on her face, he nodded in the direction of the injured man.

'How long will he be in here?'

Tess replied briefly, 'You must ask the surgeon.'

'Rather a bore,' explained the visitor,

carelessly. 'No one else can do my boots decently, y'know.' He gave a slight yawn, and added, 'No use mollycoddling them . . . They are just like animals, you know. Heal best if left alone to lick their wounds.'

Tess made no answer.

'They're all the same—malingerers, the lot of them.' He glanced indifferently at the unconscious face on the pillow. 'The blackguards will play sick, if you let 'em. Take my word for it, m'dear.' He reached out one gloved hand and placed a forefinger beneath her chin. 'What's your name?'

Tess raised her head and drew back from him as far as she was able. The scrubbing-brush was still in her hand. In silence, with lips compressed, she threw the brush with both accuracy and force into the pail of dirty water that stood at the officer's feet. There was a considerable splash, and a shower of soapy drops shot out and jetted over the impeccable trouser-legs.

He stepped back smartly. A stifled exclamation escaped him—a hot spark flared for an instant in his eyes.

Tess met him with a level gaze.

He composed his features again into their habitual bored languor, and swung upon his heel. With a clink of spur and flourish of sabretache he walked away down the length of the ward. Looking after the erect head and rigid shoulders as they passed through the entrance and out of her sight, Tess spoke under her breath on a little hiss.

'Detestable—!'

'That's Captain Hemrick, that is!' The orderly was grinning at her across the bed.

'Indeed.'

'A sight to see, ain't he?' said Grindle, with marked appreciation. 'A real toff and no mistake! Cor! Did you get an eyeful of them boots!'

Tess bent over the sick man and straightened the blankets.

'Got his own yacht here, he has, same as some of the other swells,' explained the cheerful Grindle. 'They keep them moored out in the bay, y'see, and after they've finished their day's fighting they go back on board to sleep. Just like it was a day's hunting! Why,' said Grindle, warming to his subject, 'more than half of Captain Hemrick's men was killed at Inkerman but he went back on board his yacht, they say, and sat down to his dinner, just like nothing had happened! What d'you think of that, miss?'

Tess said repressively, 'I can't waste time. Perhaps you would take away the scrubbing-water.'

December came in and brought ever-deepening snow; thick and white, it lay on the shores of Scutari and crept even to the waterline. Looking 'down on it, from the height of the eastern tower, Tess drew her cloak against the numbing cold and said with weariness,

'Well . . . the snow hides the ugliness—'

'Yes; it—at least—is clean.'

'The whole hospital is clean—as we can testify; I am sure my very bones are aching! But—but still the men are dying, Rachel! Why? Why is it so?'

Rachel said soberly, 'The men are bringing cholera with them, perhaps. It's raging in the lines—Lord Raglan has sent word that we may expect another five hundred cases. Where are they to be put? There's simply nowhere!'

Tess's face was clouded; her eyes sombre on the heavy clouds fleeing past the window.

'But even those who are not diseased—when they reach us they sicken . . . and die. As if—as if the hospital, itself, were somehow killing them.'

She rested her cheek on the window frame. Her mouth drooped; there were smudged violet shadows under her eyes.

Presently, Rachel uttered a long sigh.

'Tess . . . do you know—it is almost Christmas time.'

Tess nodded without speaking.

Rachel went on, softly.

'There will be snow in the valleys, and on Christmas Eve the singers will go out; I—

used to go with them . . . It doesn't seem real—'

'No—it isn't real. Not here—not to us . . .'

CHAPTER
FOUR

A NUN hurried into the wash-house. She searched along the rows of women at the tubs. Gliding through the noise and steam, she called urgently.

'Mrs Willett!'

Gwen Willett looked up in surprise.

'Your husband, Mrs Willett—he is in the hospital.'

Gwen's cheeks turned perfectly white.

'Is he—?'

'No, not wounded; he has taken the cholera. He is conscious, and asking for you.'

The young wife dried her reddened hands on her apron as she hastened in the nun's wake.

Thanks to the efforts of Miss Nightingale and a small army of Turkish workmen, the western tower—formerly derelict—had been hastily repaired in time to accommodate Lord Raglan's men; it was, however, far from adequate. In fact it was jammed to the rafters. There were insufficient beds, and many of the fevered men were lying on the floor; there was barely room to walk between the pallets.

Nurses were busy among them, washing lice-ridden bodies, getting them into clean shirts, coaxing them to drink. Some of the men were in delirium, or twisting double as the hideous cramps contorted them. Others lay quiescent with glazed eyes and the hectic flush of raging fever.

Rachel looked up.

'He's there, Gwen. At the end—near the wall.'

Gwen fell heavily on her knees beside her husband. Dan Willett's long legs hung over the end of the narrow mattress. The skin was pulled tight over the bones of his face. One hand plucked at the blanket that covered him, his eyes were closed.

'Danny! Danny—love!'

Gwen seized the bony hand in her own. The lad's face quivered and he opened his eyes, looking vaguely about. With a sob, Gwen stroked the black hair from his forehead, caressed the gaunt face, laid her head down on his shoulder. A ghost of a smile passed over his features. His voice was a thread.

'Is it really you, love?'

Gwen cried out urgently.

'Oh—miss! Please . . . he looks—he looks so—!'

Tess came to her side, leaning with compassion over the tear-wet face.

'Don't cry, dear Gwen. He has been lying out

in the open, you see. It has made him very weak.'

'Will he . . . is he going to—?'

'He is young, and of a strong constitution; we shall do everything we can. There is always hope, Gwen.'

The girl turned back to the pallet. She shifted her weight on her knees and bent over the colourless face.

'You will be all right—won't you, lad? And then we'll go home . . . home to Somerset.'

About to turn away, Tess paused. In an undertone, she asked, 'Did you say—Somerset?'

'Yes. Danny and I come from there; we were born in the same parish. We were married only at Easter time.'

The sick man stirred and suddenly spoke.

'Easter time.'

Gwen put her cheek against his.

'Yes, that's right, love! You remember the orchards, don't you? The apple flowers in the church? Springtime—so pretty it was . . . Danny! You will soon be well! And then we'll go home.'

He echoed faintly,

'Home.' He turned his head restlessly for a minute or two. Then his lids dropped; he appeared to doze.

His wife remained crouched beside the mattress, with his lax fingers clasped in hers. Outside the windows the daylight began to deepen into dusk. The wind was rising again, making the tower creak, and frozen drops clattered on the panes.

Rachel spoke above Gwen's head.

'Try if he will take this broth, my dear.'

Night came down beyond the window. The hours dragged by.

Tess said quietly in the girl's ear, 'Go and rest, Gwen. If he wakes, I will send for you.'

Gwen shook her head.

'Thank you, miss . . . but—but I want to be here.'

It was ten o'clock when a sudden change came over the sick man. He uttered a hoarse cry and began to toss and mutter. Gwen cried out in distress.

'His hands! They burn like fire!'

'The fever is rising again.' Tess wrung out a cloth, and began to sponge Dan Willett's face and chest. 'Do you rub his legs, Gwen; sometimes that helps to ease the cramps.'

Dan began to gasp and struggle. With heaving chest, he raised himself from the pillow. With open mouth and starting eyes, he croaked,

'Don't go back, lad—don't go back!'

Tess murmured soothingly. She slid an arm under him and supported him on her breast, passing the cool sponge over his burning skin. The dazed eyes moved around, stared, and came back to fasten on her face; but what he saw was something far beyond, far removed from the hospital ward.

A tumbled stream of words began pouring from his lips.

'There was fire—the ground all spouting up, fire, bits of men flying! Smoke—black smoke and fire—like the picture on my grandpa's wall. We used to look at it when we were boys.' He groaned. 'Boys together . . . his father's farm is next to ours . . . He went away to London—he wanted to be a surgeon; always doctorin' on the farm . . . But I knew him, all the same, the minute he came out of the smoke . . .'

He rested against her for a moment. Then he spoke again, calmly, almost conversationally.

'It was him that saved my life, you know.'

His eyes were fixed on her face. They seemed to expect a reply.

Tess asked, gently, 'Who saved you, Dan?'

There was impatience in his tone, as if he were repeating something that she ought to have known.

'Roger! Roger Verrall . . . I knew him right away—I told you—black with smoke and all! He dragged me clear—else I was a goner for sure. Then he ran back!'

For one eternal second, Tess sat perfectly still. The hand that was sponging Dan Willett's chest faltered for a moment. She made no sound.

'There was some others lying out there.' His voice began to drag, faintly, wearily. His weight sagged on her shoulder. 'He went back to the others . . . The Russkis were coming . . . It was

all black and red, and the way the bullets come
over, you'd think it was birds whistling. Something burst, right over the top . . . I saw him go
down . . . a big flash, and mud and dirt and bits
of men all up in the air like a fountain—
flying . . .'

The tired voice trailed away. His body went
limp, head lolling on her shoulder.

Very carefully she eased him to the mattress.
For a long moment she remained looking down
at his face. Then she lifted her head, and gave
Gwen a reassuring smile.

'He should sleep now, for a time.' She took
Gwen's hand and drew her to her feet. 'You must
rest now, as well; when he wakes, he will want to
see you.'

In the quiet of the nurses' quarters, Tess sat on
the edge of her cot and looked at the blank wall.

It was almost dawn, and within another two
hours she was expected back in the wards—but
she had not slept. The room was dim, and the
beds nearest to her own were empty. Farther
along, a huddled nurse snored gently, with
blankets muffled about her ears. Rain dripped
steadily, drearily, down the windows.

Tess sat motionless, staring ahead, and saw,
not the wall, but a London street on a foggy
night, deserted and dark, with the cold rising up
from the cobblestones . . . even the brisk clop of
the horses' feet seemed muffled in the fog that

smoked up from the banks of the Thames . . .
The hour was late, for Mrs Beresford's musical
soirée had been both long-drawn-out and dull,
but the luxurious interior of the carriage, with
the Cumnor crest emblazoned on its gleaming
panels, was warm and comfortable enough.
Turning her head on the velvet squabs, Tess
could see wraithlike strings of mist floating past
the windows . . . On the seat opposite to her, her
sister Lucy leaned back, yawning and complain-
ing that the muisc had been dreary—as it had, in
truth; beside her, her brother Justin sat in
silence; he was, in fact, a shade disgruntled—for
the duty of escorting his ungrateful sisters to
their evening party had cost him a jolly outing
with his cronies. Tess's mouth twitched faintly,
remembering . . .

The coachman's sudden shout of dismay as the
child darted from the darkness and fell under
their very wheels had galvanised them all with
shock. Mercifully, the little girl was not hurt, but
they could not leave her there. Justin had picked
her up from the ground and lifted her into the
carriage . . . and they had taken her home.

*Home—such a place as it was! The black rotting
tenement, the poor bare room . . . so close to the
river, so cold and dank . . . I did not know, had
never known, that people lived like that. The
broken window, and the flickering candle . . .
and a pitiful tiny baby, coughing its life away.*

Justin gave them money, for food and a phy-
sician, and we came away. But even as we left, I
knew that I would go back . . . It was still before
dawn when I slipped out of the house and re-
turned to the place . . . The baby was dead . . .
And then, while I was there, the surgeon came.

Roger Verrall.

How tired he was, tired to the bone, with his
face grave and haggard in the morning light; but
so straight and strong, with pride and courage in
every line of him. Her throat ached with bitter-
sweet tenderness as she saw again the old frock-
coat carefully brushed, the spotless rough-dried
cravat at his throat, the clean frayed cuffs that
were too short for his lean wrists . . . and his
eyes, strange, grey, the clearest she had ever
seen; they caught her and held her, so that she
could not get away . . .

Oh, yes! In that moment, even when I first saw
him, I knew.

And I told him I was a lady's maid.

Finding me there, tending the child, he took me
at first for a nurse. How easily I lied—how glibly it
came off my tongue! A lady's maid, down from
Yorkshire with 'the family' for the London season
. . . I would have told him the truth; I meant to tell
him! But the moment never came.

Sitting on the cot in the quiet nurses' room, she
sighed and trembled together, and crossed her

arms upon her breast. She looked at the drops slipping down the windowpane. Raining still . . . As it was on that last night—the night she went to tell him that she loved him.

The ring he wore . . . It was his mother's—that was the night he gave it to me. Now it lies hidden away in the dark . . . Locked away with my jewels . . . Locked in the dark, as my heart is—and shall always be . . .

It had been easy—surprisingly easy—to see him several times, stealing out of the house in the early mornings, going to the place near the river, down in the East End, to visit the child and the family in the old tenement building. But to go there at night was a different matter. Lucy had helped her and between them they had managed it; Lucy deceiving Mama, taking her sister's place at a party while Tess crept out of the house . . . The memory still gave her a twinge of guilt, but there had been no help for it.

Because Roger was to sail for the Crimea, and she loved him, and she was sure that he loved her. But she had not told him of her feelings in so many words, and it was imperative, essential, that she should do so—before he went so far away. And the plan worked perfectly! Except that Justin found out where she had gone, and followed her, and found her there.

Well . . . She blinked her gritty eyes, and

pressed her palms to the lids. It had not mattered, really; in fact, she was grateful, in a way, for Justin had helped to shield her from discovery, and had comforted her—after he had stopped being angry with her, naturally! He had instantly told Roger her real name, of course, but it had made no difference; nothing could alter her determination to have Roger Verrall for her husband. Nothing on earth would change her mind. When he returned from the Crimea, they would be married. It was as simple as that.

And—later, on a bright morning at Ribston, while she sat dreaming in the summer light with perfume and softness all about her, it was Justin who came to her across the green lawns and brought her the casualty lists.

Verrall, Roger. Surgeon. Missing—believed killed.

A long shudder went through her body. Her hot eyes grated in their sockets. She rubbed them with her knuckles.

The door of the dormitory opened softly, and Rachel's head appeared. She looked along through the shadows and saw Tess sitting upright on her bed. Flitting past the few beds which were occupied, she came up close to Tess, leaned over, and put her lips to her friend's ear.

'I am glad you are awake. I knew you would like to be told—Gwen has had her baby!'

Very slowly, from some remote place, Tess's

blank blue gaze came back, swivelled, focused on Rachel's face.

'Baby—?'

'Yes—Gwen's baby is born!'

'Oh—! When . . . ?'

'Not half an hour ago. Isn't it splendid!'

'Are they—?'

'Both well. Not the least trouble! A fine boy, too, healthy and strong!'

Tess's white lips flickered into a smile.

'That is good news! And her husband? Is he better?'

There was a silence. Rachel's eyes clouded, her sweet face fell.

'He began to sink soon after midnight . . . not so very long after you went off duty. I am afraid he is gone, love.'

Tess stared, wordless.

Rachel said, with a quivering lip, 'Gwen has not yet been told, of course. Perhaps . . . surely, the child will comfort her—make it easier for her to bear? I feel that it must be so . . .'

Tess's face suddenly crumpled. She gave a tiny moan, turned to her friend and buried her head in Rachel's breast. The hot bitter tears, too long forced back and denied, came bursting out. Her body began to shake violently under the impact of shuddering waves of grief and pain; Rachel wrapped her arms tightly about the shivering figure, crooned soft words, stroked the bright hair; but the desperate weeping went on, racking

Tess, ripping her apart. Her face was pressed against Rachel and the deep sobs were muffled, but one or two of the occupants began to stir, even in their heavy exhausted sleep.

At last, even Rachel's calm good sense began to desert her, and wild thoughts of fever, of cholera or typhus raced through her mind and frightened her. Convinced that her friend had developed an illness, she was on the point of summoning aid when the frantic sobs began at last to lessen. Gradually they eased, until at last they were reduced to an intermittent shiver that gripped Tess's body and made her teeth chatter; finally, even that died away, and she was able to sit up, draw herself together and say in a choked whisper,

'Rachel—please forgive me. I—I am rather tired.'

'Is it only that? I was afraid you were ill—'

'No.' Tess began to mop her scalding eyes.

'Are you sure?'

Tess looked up. Rachel's worried face was only inches from her own; the dark eyes fixed on her with a painful anxiety.

A long gusty sigh came suddenly from Tess's chest; it carried with it, almost involuntarily, a spate of words.

'Rachel—he is dead—I know it now. Always, before, I carried in my heart a tiny hope—but now . . . it's finished—'

'But how—what has happened?'

Tess twisted the wet handkerchief, and spoke more steadily.

'Roger was born in Somerset. His father's farm is there. When Dan Willett came into the ward last night, I learned that he was Roger's friend—their farms were close by . . . They—grew up together—' She faltered, and went on, very low,

'Dan Willet saw it happen.'

'Oh—Tess . . .'

'He saw Roger die,' Tess whispered. Her head fell forward; the features in shadow.

Rachel sat speechless, her arm about her friend.

At last Tess straightened her back, set both feet to the floor. She stood upright and moved her eyes round the room, rather blankly, as if she did not recognise it.

'He saved Dan Willet's life,' she said in a flat voice, 'and now they are both dead, after all . . . There's no sense to it . . .' She reached for Rachel's hand, and pressed it. 'Thank you, love; if you had not come, I don't know how I would have—' She swallowed hard, and lifted her arms to set her cap in place. 'I must go; it's almost time.'

'Are you fit for it?'

'Oh—! Yes. I am quite recovered—don't worry about me . . . I must leave—must go on duty.'

*   *   *

December came and went, and in the Barrack hospital the mountain of physical work undertaken by this band of women is hard to comprehend by minds geared to the necessity of labour-saving devices. With pinched-in waists and heavy skirts, armed only with buckets, mops and bar-soap, they scrubbed and scoured and rinsed, sometimes with the help of orderlies who might be coaxed or cajoled into lending a hand, but more often alone. There were four miles of wards to be cleansed on hands and knees; the old floorboards were rough and splintery, the plaster walls cracked. The women's hands were red and raw with chipped and broken nails, and the food which sustained them—broth and bread and vegetables—was adequate enough, but monotonous and restricted in an age that had never heard of vitamins. With obstinate strength they drove themselves on, and when the task was done the men in the Barrack lay in clean beds, fed and cared for, in wards as clean as female resolution and plain stubbornness could render them.

And endlessly, through the days, through the dark hours, the men were watched over; the indefatigable grey figures moved, eased, comforted—and at the small wooden table in the nurses' dormitory the tireless pen of Miss Nightingale traced on. Nothing went unobserved, nothing unrecorded—no tiny detail escaped those needle-eyes.

But the men still died.

The air became thick with death. The medical orderlies grew fearful for their own lives, and began to avoid entering the wards. The burden of their work fell on the nurses as well. The whispers stirred, and grew, and spread . . . that to come to the Barrack was to die.

Back in England, before embarking, the Scots Fusiliers and the Sixty-Third Regiment had marched through the streets to flags and colour and music. They marched cheerfully, briskly, to the beat of the drums . . . away into nothingness. By now, the Fusiliers could muster only eighty men, and of the Sixty-Third not a single man remained. In later years the learned scholars who studied the Crimean campaign estimated the numbers who melted away in the snows of that winter as sixty thousand; and of those, it was said, three-quarters were destroyed by disease.

Within the walls of the Barrack alone, nine thousand soldiers were lost in three months.

And Miss Nightingale knew why they died.

Eternally poking and probing with those steel-tipped eyes, searching and exploring into every hidden corner of the place, she knew well enough. She penetrated everywhere, looked at everything, missed nothing, and she knew that the hospital was contaminated.

The Barrack at Scutari floated in a sea of putrefaction.

The clogged and clotted drains overflowed

and washed raw filth into basements, cavities, crevices; seeping, soaking, permeating; oozing into courtyards, rising into the thickness of the walls. Water flowed into the hospital through decaying animal carcasses and rotting detritus of unnameable composition. Floors, walls, ceilings, every cranny of the place crawled with vermin and was alive with rats.

Miss Nightingale knew . . . but the army was not interested in the opinions of a Miss Nightingale. The stuffed shirts shrugged indifferent shoulders. Men died in wars; it was to be expected.

The army, however, underestimated the lady. It was back to the wooden table and the pen; the letters went home to England . . . and found their mark.

'*The entire medical service of the Army*,' ran the neat sharp handwriting, '*is in urgent need of reform. I have to do with men whose only object is to keep themselves out of blame . . .*'

In a quiet distant room, in an English castle, a pair of intent eyes studied this missive with care.

A gilded clock ticked decorously in the warm room. Cosy flames danced in a marble fireplace, and velvet curtains were drawn across tall windows that overlooked a noble park. Candlelight gleamed on smooth banded hair, pearls and soft lace, soft white hands.

A plump satin foot tapped the carpet . . . the foot slowed, and grew still, as the eyes moved over the page.

'*The gallantry of these common soldiers!*' The phrases were astringent, startling. 'Their dignity—gentleness and chivalry—in the midst of what can only be described as *the lowest sink of human misery*!'

There was silence in the warm, hushed room. The small pink mouth pursed in thought, the lips tightened.

Gravely, the smooth head nodded.

To the soft-foot servant who appeared at her elbow, the round little mouth spoke portentous words.

'Summon the Secretary at War.'

So, thanks to a stubborn lady who was awed by neither God nor devil, and certainly not by army bigwiggery, the Sanitary Commission of Engineers came to Scutari.

They did not come until February, and by then many more were dead. But they came; and when they did, they came with authority and power and the highest of Government backing.

They had one word for the Barrack hospital; *murderous*.

'Haven't I said so all along!' snapped Miss Nightingale.

As the Augean Stables were cleansed, so too was the Barrack hospital. A river, an ocean, a torrent, of limewash was sent foaming and roaring through the place. Waste and filth of every description was flushed, drained, scoured, burned or buried. The foundations, the walls, the environs, the very foreshores of the bay were cleansed and cleansed again. And when it was done, a strange thing happened. During the month of May, of every hundred men in the hospital, only five died.

It seemed like a miracle; except to Miss Nightingale, who had known all along. She had done battle with stupidity and mess and muddle, and had routed the army, out-flanked, out-manoeuvred and rolled it up, horse, foot and guns.

'It should have been done before!' bristled the lady.

Now it was Maytime in the Crimea; and another, older, miracle was happening too. The rising spring sun broke the death of winter; gradually, the deadly cold eased its grip upon the flesh. A soldier, carried across from Balaclava in a hospital ship and put to bed in the Barrack, lay resting on a pillow that smelled of soap and sun. He raised his eyes to the window and saw the golden light, blue sky, white cotton clouds. On the sill outside a bird was singing. It chirped, and fluttered, and shot away into the blue. The soldier's eyes followed its flight.

The bed in which he lay was warm, fresh and clean. His tired body was washed, and soothed by the touch of a soft white gown. A comfortable meal rested in his stomach.

The soldier rubbed his freshly-shaven chin and spoke half to himself, on a contented sigh.

'If Florence Nightingale were at our head, we'd take Sebastopol in a week.'

Tess Mainwaring said to the wife of Dan Willett, 'Gwen, what will you do now?'

The girl looked up. Her eyes were darkly rimmed and her fresh colour had faded. She smoothed the head of the child lying in her lap.

'I don't really know, miss.'

'Would you like to go home?'

'Home—! Yes, oh yes!'

Tess asked, 'May I hold him, please?'

The baby lay quietly on her breast, and looked into her face with grave eyes. She rocked him a little, marvelling at the delicacy of the skin, the purity of the flesh. She said, smiling,

'His eyes will turn brown, I think. The blue is so very deep.'

A touch of colour crept into Gwen's cheeks. Her mouth trembled.

'I do hope so—Danny's eyes were brown.'

Tess asked gently, 'You would truly like to go home to Somerset?'

'Oh—more than anything . . . I want to go back to Danny's home—only . . . . you see—'

'I understand.' Tess handed the child back to its mother. 'Now, Gwen, please listen.' She dug into a pocket and extracted a sealed letter. 'You are to travel to London. When you arrive, go immediately to the address written here and present this letter. A sum of money will then be lodged in your name and the boy's. It is sufficient to make you both secure, and my bankers will advise you on how best it may be invested.'

Gwen's eyes popped. She sat dumbfounded, open-mouthed and staring.

Tess's gaze was on the baby's face.

'I want to think of this boy growing up in the west country where his father was born . . . Is this what you wish for, Gwen?'

'I do—I do!' gasped the girl, in blank amazement. 'But miss! How can you— I don't understand!'

Tess's lips curved faintly. Wryly, half to herself, she murmured,

'There is one thing, at least, which I do not lack.' She dived again into her pocket. 'Oh—another thing, Gwen. Here is money for your fare to London.' She put a fat purse into the girl's hand.

Gwen Willett sat looking at the purse. She tried to speak—but could not.

'Dear Gwen, be happy—you and your son. He is very beautiful. One day, if it is possible, I shall hope to come into the west country, and visit you both.'

Gwen nodded fervently, still unable to find words, but smiling through the tears that began to slip down her cheeks. Tess touched the girl's hair, looked into the baby's face and turned away. At the door, she paused.

'Goodbye—I wish you both well . . .' For a moment, she hesitated, as if to say something more. Gwen waited, expectant; but Tess folded her lips, gave a nod and a last smile, and went from her sight without further word.

CHAPTER
FIVE

THE WINDOWS of the hospital wash-house stood wide to the sun. The children ran outside to catch the golden warmth on their faces. Tess plunged her arms into a frothing mass of soapsuds, and blew a cloud of glittery bubbles into the air. The sunlight caught the bubbles, and sparkled them into rainbow colours; a child who was watching leaped for them, with laughter and clapping hands.

Rachel echoed the child's trill of laughter. Dimpling, she folded the last of a huge pile of dried linen, redolent of the sun and the air.

'Mrs Matcham will be waiting for these,' she said, and heaved the basket to her hip.

'Wait just a moment and I'll help you,' Tess exclaimed. 'I am finished here.'

She hauled on the rope, and the enormous clothes-hoist with its dripping, flapping, burden rose creakingly to its full height and hung suspended. Tess took one handle of Rachel's basket. Carrying it between them, they edged between the workers at the tubs, left the wash-house and set off in the direction of the Barrack.

Their busy feet skipped along the flagged path. The basket swung ponderously between them. A brisk little breeze danced off the sparkling wavelets beyond the jetty, catching at their caps and flattening their skirts against their legs. Over their heads a bird sang, and here and there, incredible among the short green grass-tips, tiny yellow crocuses were showing. The air was crisp and blue; the wind played with the tendrils at Tess's neck, and touched Rachel's cheeks to rose.

Rachel threw back her head and drew a long, satisfying breath.

'Springtime at home! The brooks, the valleys—I'd kick up my heels like the lambs!'

'And I,' cried Tess, in a glow. 'Oh! So would I!'

They had seen horror; and it would stay with them always, for all their days. But they were young, and alive. The fresh wind, the sunlight, the fair day lifted their hearts and sent the warm vitality of their youth pulsing through their veins. Their feet flew faster. The basket teetered perilously. They giggled, guilty and breathless, and smoothed their skirts and straightened their caps before passing into the shadow of the portico which guarded the entrance to the hospital building.

They entered, and hastened away down the corridor. Neither girl noticed an officer standing there, half-concealed in an embrasure, nor would have given him a second thought if she had. They swished past him, bright-faced and busy, without a glance. From the corner of her eye Rachel glimpsed a flash of gold, a high-nosed pale countenance, a black and gold cap; but it did not register on her mind, and if it had, she would not have thought it worth mentioning.

Beneath the peaked brim of his hat, however, the eyes of Captain Travis Hemrick followed them. His gaze lingered on the slim retreating back, and the long-legged grace, of the golden-haired nurse. He watched until she turned a corner and disappeared; nor did he stir for some time but remained motionless, enigmatic eyes fixed apparently on nothing.

Some little time later, however, an observer might have noticed the Captain in close conversation with one of the orderlies; and, if sufficiently interested, might have caught a gleam of gold and a clink of coin, as money changed hands and was pocketed . . . But none of these things was remarked.

'Mrs Mainwaring. You may leave now.'

Tess murmured a word of thanks. The ward was darkened and hushed. A nurse bent above a man who stirred fretfully; other patients lay sleeping, their forms still and shadowy in the muted nightlight. Tess moved quietly to the door and left the room.

The hour was very late. The way to the nurses' quarters was deserted and rather gloomy. Out of habit, Tess walked swiftly, but she was very weary. During the afternoon the *Servern* had docked with an unexpected two hundred on board, and her normal nursing shift of twelve hours had been, as a result, considerably extended. She thought with anticipation, and a yawn, of hot soup, a clean nightgown and blessed sleep. With eyes downcast, she hurried along the hall and almost collided with the figure of an orderly, who stepped without warning in front of her.

She pulled up short with an involuntary gasp, and stared at him. He was not one of those with whom she was personally acquainted, but she had seen him occasionally about the hospital; she assumed him to be coming from a spell of duty in another part of the building.

The man stood close to her, and spoke in an urgent undertone.

'You are wanted, miss!'

Her eyes widened.

'Wanted—? What do you mean?'

'The other nurse. Your friend—Mrs Irvine.'

'I don't understand—'

'You're to come to where she is, right away—and not tell nobody.'

Tess looked at him sharply.

'I don't believe it.'

The man's heavy face was impassive.

'She's outside the hospital, miss. In the wash-house.'

Poised to brush by him, Tess gazed in astonishment.

'Impossible! Mrs Irvine is presently on duty in the wards!'

'No, she's not, miss. She's outside, in the wash-house. And you're to come.'

Tess turned to hurry away, yet paused, irresolute.

The man took a step towards her and spoke with stronger emphasis.

'She—your friend—was crying, miss.'

Tess swung round with open mouth.

'She wants you straight away,' the orderly urged.

'*Crying*—! Good God! Whatever can be wrong!'

'I don't know, miss. That's all I know.'

Tess drew a sharp breath and hesitated no longer.

'She is alone in the wash-house, you say?'

'Yes, miss. Waiting for you.'

Tess said with decision, 'I shall go at once.'

The orderly nodded, and melted into the gloom.

With pounding heart, Tess began to flit along various corridors and side-passages, working her way towards the rooms which comprised the hospital kitchens; these led one into the other, and opened from an outside door on to a path that led to the wash-house. Anxiety had banished her fatigue. Frantically she cast about for any possible reason that could have taken Rachel to the distant and deserted wash-house in the middle of the night—she could think of none.

Something terrible indeed must have occurred to cause such behaviour, but whatever it might be—no matter in what state of distress she might find Rachel—one thing was clear. The immediate, the urgent, necessity was to find her friend and bring her safely back within the hospital walls before the absence of either one of them should be remarked. For any nurse to be caught outside at that hour would mean instant dismissal and public shame; the prospect was not one to be relished.

Tess stole through the cavernous empty kitchens, holding her breath, keeping to the wall. On one of the hobs a giant broth-kettle simmered, a dozing cookhand sat nodding near the fire. No one else was about. Gliding from one patch of shadow to the next, Tess reached the outer door, unlatched it inch by inch, and slipped through.

She flattened herself against the wall and looked about. All was quiet.

With a sigh of relief, she gathered her skirts around her knees and set off in haste along the path. The wash-house building lay some hundred yards from the Barrack. At this hour it was dark, silent and deserted; nothing stirred as she hurried towards it. The air was still and cold, and there was no moon. The sound of water lapping about the jetty came to her, and she thought a shadow moved, somewhere near the shore. When she looked in that direction, however, there was nothing to be seen.

Breathing a little faster, she came to the dark building. The entrance loomed before her. She paused, and put a hand to the door. She could hear nothing within; hesitating, she wondered if she had misunderstood, or had the orderly mistaken Rachel's message?

To her surprise, however, the door—which ought to have been fastened—gave under her touch. She swung it open, and stepped inside.

The vast room was a cave of weird shadows and darkness. The rows of blankets and garments hanging overhead seemed to move, eerily pale in the blackness, although commonsense insisted that it could not be so—the windows were shut, and there were no draughts to stir the air. She stood just inside the door, and peered about. Her sharp eyes searched and probed, travelling to the further end past the great black bulk of the boilers, and there she discerned a faint glow, and a thin bar of light as if from a shaded lantern, falling across the floorboards.

Tess took a step forward, and called softly.

'Rachel . . . Are you there?'

The whispering echoes from under the roof brought a high-pitched thread of sound to her straining ears.

'I am here . . .'

She waited no longer. Moving briskly into the room, she began to make her way between benches and empty upturned tubs, her eyes fixed on that beckoning glow of light. She called again, in a louder, urgent tone.

'Rachel! Where are you? You must—'

A blacker shadow stirred in the darkness and detached itself from the background. A form materialised behind her, an arm snaked about her waist. She stiffened, and gasped aloud.

A voice that was of a certainty not Rachel's, with distinct and mocking amusement in its drawling cadences, spoke into her ear.

'Here I am, m'dear!'

Swift and lithe, Tess swung about within the encircling arm, and found herself looking into the smiling countenance of Captain Hemrick.

For a minute, shock and disbelief held her rigid.

The Captain's mouth was only inches from her own. The lantern beam was enough to illumine his polished hair and moustache. His hard black eyes glimmered, and little flickers of gold reflected from his uniform. His smile broadened, and his teeth flashed under the oiled moustache.

'By George! Y'know, you really are a beauty,' he said.

Cold shock receded and gave way to furious outrage. She began to struggle, fighting to free herself, striking with both fists at his chest. It was useless.

The arm about her waist was heavy and iron-hard; it tightened, clamping her to his body. He laughed, and leaned even closer. His free hand gripped her chin, forcing her face upwards and towards the light. He searched her features with avid, gleaming eyes.

'You aren't going to get away! Be quiet, and listen to me. My yacht is moored out in the bay, there's a boat waiting at the jetty. We'll be well away by morning.'

She grew very still.

'I want you,' he said. His breath was hot on her face. 'What d'you wish to stay here for—scrubbing floors? I can offer you better than that! You shall live aboard the *Dancer*, with wine and food and comfort. And after—when we are back in England—'

Tess stared at him mutely. Deliberately, by calculated degrees, she allowed her body to relax, to grow soft . . . Ever so slightly, in seeming acquiescence, she drooped towards him. Her lips fell apart.

In unconscious response, the bruising grip on her waist began to slacken. His arm loosened and grew lax, as he continued,

'Ah . . . I thought that would please you! When we reach England—you shall have whatever your fancy chooses. Gowns, jewels, your own carriage. Come with me now!'

She kept her gaze on his; her silence implied consent. He saw the dusky fire smouldering in those deep and dreamy eyes, and totally misread it. Her long fingers were crisping into talons; he did not notice.

He began to breathe faster.

'You're a tasty morsel—by God you are!' he panted. 'You have teased me since first I clapped eyes on you . . . you witch! We'll seal the bargain, eh? And then—'

She closed her eyes, as if in rapture, and swayed towards him. He removed the encompassing arm and slid his hands to her shoulders.

'One kiss . . .' He whispered. His red full-lipped mouth touched her own.

Like a spring released Tess exploded into action.

A sharp elbow, with all her strength behind it, drove full into his throat. Almost in the same moment, she slashed both hands across his face. The nails stung his skin like a whiplash.

Hemrick was caught entirely by surprise.

Tess thrust him sharply away and sprang backwards out of his reach. The hapless Captain staggered a little. The backs of his knees came in contact with an empty tub; he sat down suddenly, with an undignified thump. Collapsed in disarray, with hat tipped forward and jangle of spurs, he was momentarily helpless.

With eyes blazing, Tess launched a furious kick at her discomfited adversary; her boot connected with a gratifying clunk. Then she whirled about and ran for the door. Nimbly she dodged and swooped between the benches. By the time Hemrick had scrambled to his feet, she had gained the entrance.

He glimpsed her figure against the sky as she flashed through the doorway, then she vanished in the darkness. He heard the diminishing sound of her running feet on the path.

She had not, he realised, vouchsafed him a single word.

Tess raced with beating heart for the sanctuary of the hospital walls. She was shaking, but not with fear; her feelings were compounded of humiliation, embarrassment and healthy wholehearted fury. Her entry into the kitchens and her passage towards the nurses' quarters were more precipitate than her exit had been; by good fortune, however, she met nobody.

She plumped herself on her cot and sat with flaming cheeks and clenched fists, glaring in front of her. Fool—fumed Tess—fool! To be taken in by so stupid a trick! As if I should not have known that Rachel would never, never—! She realised, as she cooled a little, that the man could not possibly have carried her off by actual force. Any attempt to coerce a kicking scream-ing victim on board his wretched yacht would have created a fine disturbance and resulted in her speedy rescue. No! She had been in no

physical danger . . . But what raised her ire—
what she resented so strongly—was his blatant,
selfish disregard of the consequences to herself,
had she been impelled to shriek for help.

She would have been expelled from Miss
Nightingale's service and sent home in disgrace.
No explanation, no excuses, would have been
accepted. And rightly so, seethed Tess, for who
would believe me idiot enough to be duped by a
story so clumsy, so childish, so—! Tess gritted
her teeth . . . And that creature had actually
thought—had expected—that I, Tess Mainwaring, would . . . Oh! It was too much!

At last, however, she gave a heavy sigh. She
raised her arms and unpinned the cap from her
braids. A little ruefully, she looked at her pock-
et-watch. The hour was long past midnight; before too few hours had passed, she must be back
on the wards. She shrugged off her worsted
jacket, bent to remove her shoes and straightened up wearily. The day had been protracted,
and even her young strength was depleted.

The recent incident had been both stupid and
tiresome but, yawning widely, she decided to
dismiss the ridiculous incident from her mind. It
was futile, after all, to waste one's energy in
anger. True, she had been deceived like a
silly child, but there was, in the event, no harm
done.

A brief recollection of the resplendent
Captain sprawled in dishevelment atop an

empty wash-tub flickered to her mind; her lips twitched.

Tess yawned again, even wider, her head touched the pillow. She fell off the edge of a cliff into bottomless sleep.

Left in sole and undisputed possession of the wash-house, Travis Hemrick straightened his shako and swore.

A vicious rage began to swell in him. He put a hand to his smarting face—the fingers came away wet. He shook his head, and cursed with fervour and energy.

The girl's reaction to his advances stunned him; he could scarcely comprehend such audacity. To be so flouted by a common nurse! A girl spawned, most probably, in a back-slum! And he had been ready to bestow his favours upon her . . . The insolence of her behaviour made him splutter. It was some minutes before he could master his anger and resume his customary mask of indifference. Then, in a dignified manner, he made his way through the quiet night towards the jetty, strolling its length with a deliberately measured gait. Dark water was racing beneath the timbers. The small rowboat which was tied up at the landing-stage rocked and bumped in the swell.

In silence, the Captain seated himself in the dinghy and was rowed out towards the place where his yacht rode at anchor in the freshening breeze. If the servant who plied the oars noticed his master's discomfiture, or permitted himself a discreet grin, he was careful not to let it be seen. Captain Hemrick's lackeys were well aware of the consequences of their master's temper.

The silence continued, and was preserved unbroken, as the owner of the dainty sailing vessel mounted to her deck. Hemrick muttered an order to his sailing-master, and withdrew to the privacy of his hushed and luxurious saloon. Here the sight of an inviting supper-table set for two, with delicate crystal and napery and silver, met his eye upon entering; it did not, however, appear to give him any marked degree of pleasure. The servant who hovered in readiness was banished with a growl, and did not stay to question, but withdrew in noiseless haste.

Travis Hemrick threw himself into a velvet-padded armchair. He lit a cheroot, and slumped back with legs outstretched and brows lowered, staring through the porthole. Waves slapped the *Dancer*'s graceful sides; ropes and tackle creaked as sails were hoisted and anchor weighed. Running before the rising wind, the sleek craft stood out to sea.

In the saloon, Hemrick sat on; morosely staring in blank, frowning silence at the dark water rippling past.

He had expected gratitude and had been treated with loathing. It was a new and unpalatable experience. He was handsome, well-born and rich; very much accustomed to having his person admired and his wishes gratified, and to thinking highly of his achievements as conqueror of the weaker sex. To be thus summarily dismissed by a girl to whom he had offered the privilege of his attentions and an escape from drudgery to a life of luxury and pleasure was even now almost impossible for him to comprehend. He lifted the decanter at his elbow, and knitted his brows.

Damn the stupid chit! What could be the matter with her! He drained the glass and refilled it, conscious of a resentment that still seethed. Under the dashing moustache his mouth took on an ugly twist. The glass was emptied and filled again.

True to her name, the yacht spread her wings and danced out to sea; white water foamed behind her. The level in the decanter grew lower as the minutes slid by into an hour. Gradually, as the brandy mounted to his brain, the Captain's anger began to dull; as the night wore on, anger was replaced, and superseded, by feelings of strong bewilderment.

For, try as he would, he could not account for the girl's rejection of him. He considered the incident from every angle, and the longer he thought about it the more puzzled he became. He found himself totally at a loss. The cheroot smouldered down and singed his fingers; he threw the stub upon the carpet and stamped on it. Well! It was a pity—a damned pity! The slut had proved herself to be a hellcat, but he had no objection to that. In fact, he preferred it—some temper sauce improved the flavour! In his mind's eye he looked her over again . . . He really could not remember having seen a more enticing shape; and as for her face . . .

Travis Hemrick's thoughts came to an abrupt halt.

Slowly, he straightened in his chair and sat upright.

That face—!

With absent care, he set down the brandy glass.

Eyes intent, he re-lived the moment when he had turned her to the light and studied her features. In retrospect, he examined again, and made note of, each contour, and from the jumble of his somewhat brandy-ridden thoughts an image—an expression—came suddenly to the fore, and retreated, teasing. He made an effort and summoned it back, trying to fix it in his mind; took a sharp breath, forced himself to concentrate—the image flickered, and mocked him.

What was it—*who* was it, mirrored in the lineaments of that face which he had searched so lingeringly, there in the glow of a lantern in that empty building? His brows drew together. His eyes were shining black slits between puckered lids; half-seen, half-remembered, the picture

rose again . . . Her name, too, there was something there—the obliging orderly had discovered
it for him. The name—what was it?

The Captain's eyes flew suddenly open. He
reared up in his chair.

'By God!'

A low whistle came from his lips. He got up
and began to stride about the room. His brain
raced and his breath came faster; and in a start-
ling instant, on a thought that was entirely free of
any clouding effects of brandy, he knew whose
was the face which so strongly resembled that of
a female nurse in the Barrack hospital.

Hemrick stopped short in the middle of the
carpet and gave a triumphant shout.

'*Mainwaring*!'

Standing quite still, with a mind that was
perfectly clear, he sorted back through the years
of his life, flipping them aside like the pages of a
book; finding the one he sought.

He saw himself, as a schoolboy, a member of
the lordly Sixth, and beyond himself, far down in
a lower form of the school, a certain stubborn,
impertinent brat . . . one Justin Mainwaring.
Mainwaring—Cumnor's heir! Oh! I remember
him! And I'll be bound he hasn't forgot me
either, thought the Captain, vindictively. Obstinate little red-headed beast—is he grateful, I
wonder, for the trouble I took to try and teach
him his manners . . .

Mainwaring! That's who she looks like!

And now I know who she is. She is fairer in colouring than her brother the Viscount, but the likeness is amazing for all that! There's no mistaking it.

Rather slowly, Captain Hemrick returned to the armchair and seated himself. Half under his breath, savouring the syllables, he spoke her name.

'The Lady Eustacia Mainwaring.'

Daughter to the Earl of Cumnor, Viscount Mainwaring's sister, and . . . one of England's greatest heiresses.

Leaning back in the chair, eyes half-closed, he recalled the affair very well. He had been abroad during that London season, but the story had reached his ears—which was not surprising. It had been a nine days' wonder.

The Lady Eustacia Mainwaring—acclaimed beauty—darling of the debutante set; apparently on the point of capturing one of the season's most brilliant matrimonial prizes . . . Weatherall, wasn't it? Dullest of dogs, but the catch of the year—suitable in every way!

And then—!

Yes, indeed, it had caused quite a furore in the rarefied air of the first circles. The girl had thrown the lot to the winds, and declared her fixed intention of becoming—of all things—a common nurse. Unimaginable! But she had done it!

And now—she was here. A hospital nurse in

the Barrack at Scutari. The Lady Eustacia . . . Cumnor's daughter.

Travis Hemrick sat very still. At last, with an air of thoughtfulness and a hand that was perfectly steady, he extracted another cheroot from his cigar-case. Lighting it with care, he watched the smoke rise and wreath before his face; his chin sank to his chest.

The Carfax fortune, wasn't it?

Settled equally on Cumnor's two daughters— twins, weren't they? The other girl had married in her first season. The money came to them through their mother, he remembered; Lady Cumnor—the sole inheritor of the staggering Carfax wealth. As the smoke trickled from his lips, the mouth of Travis Hemrick began to curl into a smile. A light grew in his eyes—keen, speculative . . . an expression almost beatific crept over his countenance. His white fingers beat a gentle tattoo on the polished armrest.

Well! Her furious rejection of his proposition need no longer trouble him—that was now perfectly explained!

His wounded vanity was instantly healed and the Captain's mind began to play with the tantalising thought of that enormous fortune. Never touched—for Cumnor himself was as rich as Croesus, all the world knew—all that money, busily accumulating and adding to itself down the years . . . A trickle of excitement ran through him.

He had himself been born to wealth and luxury, but his own inheritance paled when compared with what would come to the Lady Eustacia. Besides—the necessities of life were damned expensive; his horses, his racing bets— endless demands from tailors and wine- merchants . . . gambling debts. A man had to live . . .

All that money—here! Ripe fruit for the picking!

And then, of course, there was the lady herself.

His cheeks still burned from the scratches she had dealt him. He rubbed his face thoughtfully. A shrew—a termagant—but that did not matter. He smiled a little. Spirit was desirable in a woman; it added zest to the taming process. The Lady Eustacia would learn to run in harness. The thought afforded him a pleasant anticipatory thrill.

Skipping before the wind, the *Dancer* held course for Balaclava Bay. In the saloon, Travis Hemrick relaxed, head on cushion, eyes half- closed. His face was quite composed, but behind the cool façade his brain was far from abstracted. With the cold calculation that was characteristic of him when bent on furthering his own ends, the Captain gave himself diligently to thought.

CHAPTER
SIX

STANDING AT the stove, stirring a pot of gruel, Rachel looked up as Tess's head appeared at the door.

'Rachel—what do you think? I am to go on a voyage!'

Rachel put down the ladle.

'A voyage! Good heavens!'

Tess bounded to her side.

'It will be quite an adventure! All the way across to Balaclava—the letter, you see, was a little delayed, and now that she has received it, naturally she wishes to make up for lost time—and so—'

'Tess—dear Tess!' Rachel burst out laughing. 'I don't understand a word you are saying! A voyage—a letter? Explain, I beg of you!'

'The letter—'

'Tess! What letter?'

'It's from the War Office. You know that Miss Nightingale had previously been barred from visiting Balaclava. Well—! Permission has come! She is to inspect the hospitals there, and make what changes she thinks fit. Her orders are to be immediately carried out!'

'She has been given full authority?' Rachel was awed. 'That is a triumph indeed!'

'Yes! And the letter was dispatched a month ago, but it has only just arrived. That is why we are to set out at first light tomorrow. With this fine weather, we ought to reach the Bay in just a few days.'

'Good gracious! That is certainly very exciting!' Rachel gave the gruel a turn or two with the ladle, and sent her friend a rather thoughtful look. 'You know, Tess,' she said slowly, 'Miss Nightingale does not look well; I have noticed it particularly in recent days. It's to be hoped that this new undertaking won't prove too much for her.'

'She is over-tired—that's true.' Tess nodded. 'I am sure it is not to be wondered at! Perhaps the journey will refresh her? At least, while we are on board, she may rest for a time.'

'Mmm . . . you are right there.'

'Two of the cooks are to go, and some orderlies and half a dozen nurses. I only wish—' She stopped, and a cloud passed over her face. She looked into her friend's eyes, and went on rather sadly, 'I do wish, love, that you were coming with me. I—I had hoped that we might stay together.'

'I shall miss you,' Rachel replied, with a sigh. 'But it cannot be helped. After all,' she pointed out, with her usual commonsense, 'we cannot all go. Some must remain here.'

'I suppose so. Mrs Matcham will take control of the Barrack; Mrs Thiele is to accompany us.'

Rachel stirred the pot briskly, and dimpled.

'Watch out for stray bullets, now! Those hospitals are close to the lines!'

Tess threw her arms about the other girl and planted a kiss on Rachel's smooth cheek, saying earnestly,

'I shall miss you dreadfully, love!'

Rachel returned the kiss and responded to the hug with fervour.

'And I you! Perhaps you will not be away so *very* long!'

Tess said soberly, 'Rachel. You have become my true friend. I am grateful for it.'

'I feel that, too,' answered Rachel, with a steadfast look. 'I hope that I may always be your friend, Tess.'

'Of that,' said Tess, 'you may be very sure.' She took Rachel's hand. 'I must go; I have night duty, and we leave at first light . . . Good-bye, dear Rachel, I'll write at the first possible moment.'

They exchanged a final warm embrace; with a heartfelt squeeze of Rachel's hand, Tess darted to the door. She looked back to smile, gave a brief wave, and sped away.

In the bitter storms of the winter past, ships had taken two weeks to bring the wounded across from Balaclava Bay, but the passage of Miss

Nightingale and her party over the summer waters was both swift and exhilarating. The yacht which was provided to convey them from Scutari was fast and trim-rigged. It flew before a spanking wind. Their cabins were snug, and the decks, wet in the mornings with sparkling dew, dried white in the sun. Standing at the rail with the breeze whipping her hair, Tess exclaimed,

'Oh, Grindle—how good this is! I feel young again!'

The old man looked with admiration at the vivid face, and the blue eyes that danced like the sun-flecked waves.

'Well, now—I wouldn't have said you were so very old, miss,' he grinned.

Her eyes darkened; she veiled them with her lashes.

'I have felt so . . . at times. When there were so many whom we could not help . . .'

'Don't think like that,' the orderly said. 'What you have to do, always, is think about the ones that live.'

Her eyes widened a little. She studied his face.

'You are very right,' she said at last. 'Someone else—once—reminded me of that . . .' She added, after a pause, 'Grindle. I am glad you are with me. I—have come quite to rely on you, do you know that?'

'Thank yer,' said Grindle, rather gruffly, staring at the sea. They stood together at the rail in comfortable silence.

Suddenly, Grindle cast a hunted look over his shoulder, gave Tess a sidelong look and spoke in a hasty undertone.

'Strike a light! I'm orf! See yer later, miss!'

Tess smothered a smile and turned to greet Mrs Thiele, as that lady advanced in her stately way along the deck. She paused beside Tess and asked pleasantly,

'Are you enjoying the air, Mrs Mainwaring?'

'Oh, yes—indeed, ma'am.'

Eyes on the sunny waves, Mrs Thiele mused,

'It is certainly most refreshing. We have journeyed very quickly—the boat should reach Balaclava tomorrow.'

'So soon? We have been sailing only three days.'

'Yes.' The keen, kind eyes of the senior nurse lingered on the wake behind them. She stifled a sigh. 'I only wish . . .'

Tess hesitated, and then asked, with some diffidence,

'You seem—a little anxious, ma'am. Is there some way in which I may be of help?'

Mrs Thiele pursed her lips.

'She will not rest. Even now she remains in her cabin, working, writing—I cannot persuade her to walk on deck and take the air. And—she is so weary . . .'

Tess said quietly, 'We have noticed it.'

'These past months have undermined her strength—and when we reach Balaclava, there will be fresh tasks to be faced.' The older woman's eyes were filled with concern. 'She takes no care for her own health—her only thought is for the work that she has to do!'

'I know,' Tess said humbly. 'I—we—are all sensible of it.'

Mrs Thiele's fine eyes softened.

'You are a good girl. I have watched you; you, and your friend Mrs Irvine. The youngest two among us—and you have both done well.' She studied Tess's face. 'I have to confess that in your case I had doubts . . . Your comparative inexperience, together with your background—I did not think that you would be able to—However!' She smiled warmly. 'Happily, I was mistaken, and gladly admit to it. Enjoy the journey, nurse! There will be a great deal to do, I dare say, when we arrive tomorrow.'

The lady departed, treading the deck with a certain smooth gracefulness, despite the proportions of her ample figure.

A conspiratorial croak sounded in Tess's ear.

'Whatser matter? She jaw you out?'

Rather pink about the ears, Tess murmured, 'No . . . She was—kind.'

Grindle guffawed.

'Kind! Get away! You oughter hear what she says to me!'

Tess said, with a twinkle, 'Then you must take care to do things as she wishes.'

Grindle assumed an expression of exaggerated gloom.

'Hounded by females on every side,' he said, mournfully. 'A man ain't got no peace. If she don't tell me off, then I know for sure you will!'

Tess laughed; the orderly joined in.

Presently she asked, 'Have you a family in England, Grindle? A home?'

'Well—no.' He looked straight ahead. 'Y'see, lass, I've been a soldier all me life. Joined at sixteen; been all over, here and there. The place I call my 'ome is an army barracks.'

'But this time you will be discharged, won't you?'

'That's right. A man gets old, y'know!'

Under her lashes, Tess sent him a long speculative glance. However, she said no more.

Mrs Thiele's prediction was correct. At Balaclava, there was a great deal to be done.

There were five field hospitals, strung along the shores of the Bay. Wounded men came to these straight from the battle lines, to be given emergency treatment or patched up to face the three hundred miles across the Black Sea to Scutari. There were no women at Balaclava—no wives, no children. The staff was composed of surgeons, ex-soldiers who served as orderlies and such walking wounded as were able to lend a hand in caring for their comrades before returning to the trenches.

These hospitals won some approval from Miss Nightingale. She acknowledged their difficulties, and during the days of inspection she awarded a certain measure of praise to the efforts that had been made, under circumstances which could only be described as trying.

There was much, however, that did not please her. The list of amendments, improvements, instructions grew steadily longer. The construction of entirely new kitchens was immediately begun; better food—more linen, blankets, utensils, supplies—and, as always, cleanliness . . . the first requirement. The entire party plunged into work, for no delay was brooked—all that was wrong must instantly be set to rights. Very soon, the daily round of the nurses became almost indistinguishable from their routine at Scutari.

There was one important difference, however—and that lay in the manner of their reception at the Bay.

The contrast with their first arrival at Scutari was marked. They were met as the boat docked, and welcomed; their baggage was carried ashore. They themselves were conducted to quarters where rather touching efforts had been made to provide some sort of comfort. The nurses' dormitory boasted two chairs, a cupboard (slightly unsteady) and even a cracked mirror on the wall. Both Miss Nightingale and Mrs Thiele were given the luxury of rooms of their own. Someone had found an enamel mug and had actually gathered a bunch of bright crocuses to put in it.

'Why! We might almost be guests,' said Tess, wondering.

Mrs Thiele replied with a certain grimness.

'Not before time! It is all due to her . . . She has won respect for us.'

The weather at Balaclava was bright and pleasantly warm. In the trenches the fighting was sporadic, while crowned heads and strategists (for the most part far away) wrangled, and debated, and planned the next moves of the great chess game, with men as pawns. It was possible, therefore, for Miss Nightingale's orders to be promptly carried out, and her projects speedily implemented.

The chief surgeon, Mr Crockford, was normally inclined to an irritability of temperament; it was almost amusing to observe the deference and the alacrity with which he hastened to smooth the path of Miss Nightingale. No female nurse had set foot on Balaclava before, but if there were any grumblings among the male staff at this arbitrary invasion of feminine authority into their domain, these were suppressed. No dissension overtly arose; the tenor of the days seemed almost placid.

'One could nearly imagine,' remarked Tess wistfully, 'that this dreary war is finished.'

'Well it ain't,' Grindle said forthrightly. 'Nor it

won't be—not until they take Sebastopol, no matter what. The news is that they are massing to try for the Great Redoubt. Things'll get hot again before it's over, miss.'

'I suppose you are right . . . But just now, one could almost pretend that the war—if not over— will soon be so.'

The following morning, however, when she entered the ward for duty at eight o'clock, it was no longer possible to pretend. During the small hours, a soldier had been brought in with a ghastly stomach wound. Just watch him, the surgeon told her briefly; nothing to be done.

Tess approached the bed.

She was shocked by the extreme youthfulness of the face on the pillow. Since the heavy losses of the winter, she had become accustomed to seeing ever younger soldiers among the reinforcements arriving at the front; but this boy, she thought, could barely have reached his sixteenth birthday. She saw, with sadness, that he was conscious. She fetched another pillow and raised his head a little. His eyes followed her movements, turning from side to side.

He shifted his arms about on the blanket and began to struggle for speech. The voice rasped thickly, but at last a word issued from his throat.

'Water—'

She leaned over him, stroking his face, and shook her head.

The rule that prevailed throughout the hospital was laid down—all-embracing and immutable. Under no circumstances was a man with abdominal or stomach injuries allowed to drink.

Pity stabbed through her. His eyes were desperate. Gently, knowing it to be a lie, she said,

'You will be better soon. Then you may have water.'

Suddenly, the boy heaved himself up from the pillow. He raised an imploring arm; she followed his eyes, and saw with dismay that on a table close by someone had placed a mug filled with water. He reached towards it . . . the moan that came from his lips tore at her heart.

Tess looked round in despair; there was no one in sight.

She thought, trying to be cool, trying to reason . . . He is going to die. He is tormented by thirst. If I break the rule, he will die, just the same . . . but it will be easier, perhaps. Why should he suffer to no purpose?

The cup was near by. She picked it up—the burning gaze followed the movement of her hand. She held the water to his lips.

The lad gulped and gulped, open-mouthed. When she took away the cup it was empty.

A change came over him then. He sank back on the pillow, and looked straight at her, wide-eyed. He framed some hoarse words. They were faint, but clearly audible.

'Ellen! I knew you would come—'

Tess took his hands and held them tight.

'Ellen love—kiss me . . .'

She bent her head and softly laid her lips on the poor cracked mouth. He drew a fluttering breath; gave a little smile; and ceased to breathe.

Tess released the quiet hands and stood looking down at him. She wished that somehow, somewhere, the girl whose name was Ellen could know what comfort her unseen presence had given to a lad in his dying.

At her elbow, the surgeon spoke.

'When did he die?'

'Only a minute or two ago, sir.'

Crockford's gaze fell on the empty cup. He stiffened; his long nose quivered like a terrier's.

He turned on her so suddenly that she flinched a little.

'You!' he hissed. 'You gave him water!'

'Sir—his thirst was terrible—'

'You have killed him!'

She faltered through blanched lips, 'Sir . . . He was dying—'

Crockford brought his face close to hers. His expression was malevolent.

'And so—*you* hastened his death!'

For the remainder of her hours of duty Tess felt lifeless and cold. It was as if she had received a blow from which the numbness had not yet passed. Dully, she wondered if the surgeon would complain of her to Miss Nightingale and concluded that he would probably do so; even that prospect evoked no response in her; she

could not feel that it mattered. Walking back to
her quarters at last with rather dragging steps,
she encountered Mrs Thiele in the hall.

The senior nurse glanced sharply at her.

'What's the matter, nurse?'

'I—I . . . that is, nothing, ma'am; I—'

She was taken firmly by the elbow and ushered
into Mrs Thiele's room. The door was closed;
with her characteristic brevity, the lady ordered,

'Don't quibble. Sit down and tell me.'

Tess could never have imagined herself con-
fiding in one so imperturbable, so undemonstra-
tive. But, all the same, there was something very
reassuring, after all, in Mrs Thiele's aspect. Her
level gaze, as she held the girl's eyes with her
own, was filled with the wise knowledge of many
things seen through the long years . . . and remembered.

Tess's face crumpled.

'He said that I killed him!' The tears spilled
over. 'It was cruel—not to let him drink!
Cruel—' sobbed Tess.

The story came tumbling out.

Gravely, without interrupting, Mrs Thiele
listened to the end. At length—

'You were very wrong, Mrs Mainwaring, to
disobey a surgeon's rule.'

Tess bit her lip and twisted her hands together.

'I must have your assurance,' went on the
measured voice, 'that such a thing will not occur
again.'

Tess whispered, 'You have it, ma'am.'

There was a pause. Tess continued to regard her hands. Looking at the downcast face, Mrs Thiele spoke again, in quite a different tone.

'However! I am not afraid to admit to you, nurse, that given the circumstances you have described, I myself would have done exactly the same thing.'

Tess looked up, incredulous.

'There must, of course, be rules,' said Mrs Thiele, meditatively. 'Otherwise there would be a sad lack of order. I am of the opinion, nevertheless, that there are times when rules should be laid aside.' A large and capable hand reached out and patted Tess firmly on the shoulder. 'You are a nurse, Mrs Mainwaring, and there is no rule or regulation that I know of which forbids a nurse to show compassion.'

In a jumble of confusion and gratitude, Tess stammered her thanks and got herself out of the room. The surgeon's vindictive words were hurtful still, but the words of Mrs Thiele overlay them, and warmed her heart, and remained with her.

She had caused a man to die quickly . . . but still she saw, and continued to see, a boy's wide eyes, going out into the dark . . . and in those eyes, the look of peace.

CHAPTER
SEVEN

'MISS! THE Frenchies are bombarding the outer works of Sebastopol,' Grindle informed Tess chattily. 'There's more than four hundred big guns firing at the north face, so I hear—that is, counting ours as well.'

'Oh, yes?' Tess said absently. She was looking, Grindle thought, a mite drooping. His keen eyes picked out the darkness under her eyes. He spoke bracingly.

'Now, miss! You just cheer up! One last big shemozzle and then it's all over; you'll see!'

She smiled slightly but made no reply. Grindle followed as she moved to the next bed. Its occupant was sleeping. Tess observed him with a frown of concentration.

'By the way,' Grindle said behind her, 'I didn't tell you the news, yet, did I?'

The sleeping man was broad and heavily built. Tess slid both arms under him and braced herself against his weight.

'I'll give you a hand to turn him, miss.'

'Thank you.'

Between them they levered the soldier over

and eased him on his side. The bedclothes were turned back over the foot of the cot. She reached for them, and Grindle obligingly took the opposite side.

As she smoothed the blankets over the man's shoulder, the orderly continued to talk. The monologue of his voice flowed past her.

'. . . and after all this time!' Grindle was saying. 'Whoever would have thought it? Both of them given up long ago for dead . . .'

Some pieces of lint had fallen to the floor. She bent to gather them.

'Found their way to Odessa, they did, hiding in the daytime. Stole a boat—and then, they came all that way around by sea—Lord knows how they wasn't drowned! Round past Kamiesh they came, with only one sail, and fetched up on the coast, not far from the old monastery.'

Tess knitted her brows.

'That arm must be re-dressed; but perhaps he ought to sleep first . . .'

'Ain't it a small world, though! The very man that Dan Willett seen—it's him for sure!'

'I need fresh bandages, Grindle. Would you get them?'

'Right, miss. You remember Willett, don't you? The lad who died, that time in Scutari? Spoke of a surgeon he saw at Alma. This is the same man—it must be! The surgeon and a Hussar, Major Melrose, have been all this time in the

Russki jail, away over at Tirespol! Ain't you heard about it?'

There was no reply. Tess had turned to the next bed. Grindle talked on to her unheeding back.

'No, you wouldn't have heard; you've been in here all day. Well! This pair strolled into Head-quarters at daylight—reported for duty, calm as you please! The Hussar has got a busted leg, and the other's had his head split open—and they're both a bit starved, like—but they're all right. Old Croaky goggled a treat when these two informed him that the Russian doctors ain't half bad. Pair of cool cards, the both of 'em, if you ask me!'

Tess looked over her shoulder, and met his expectant twinkle.

'If—by "old Croaky"—you refer to the head surgeon, Grindle,' she began, in mock severity. She laid a hand on the patient's chest, and listened for his breathing; without particular interest, she added, 'Did you say something about an escape?'

The orderly looked at her with deep reproach.

'Miss—! You ain't been listening!'

'I was thinking of other things,' Tess apologised. She began to roll a length of unused bandage. Glancing at the little man, she realised that he was genuinely disappointed. In quick contrition, she said,

'I am truly sorry, Grindle; I am a little preoccupied today. Please tell me again what has happened.'

'The Hussar is over at general Headquarters; the surgeon turned up here, a couple of hours ago!'

Tess's hands went still. Slowly, she turned her eyes to him, and fastened them on his face.

Something of his unheeded narrative—phrases, disjointed fragments—floated to the surface of her mind. Her mouth opened; she stared wordless at the puckered face across the bed.

'They've been in the Russian jail—'

She uttered a gasp. A trickle that was both hot and cold at once ran through her vitals. Staring, half-stifled, she whispered,

'I—don't understand—'

'The surgeon, miss! The one Dan Willett saw! Verrall—that's his name . . . Here—*miss!*'

He scurried round the bed-end and caught her by the waist.

'Hold up, miss—steady on!'

Tess's knees buckled. She sagged forward, Grindle held her bodily against him; they were the same height; her head lolled across his shoulder, helpless as a rag doll's.

'Christ! What's the matter?' In consternation, he looked around. There was nobody by. The girl's face was ashen—her eyes rolled upwards.

Grindle grabbed the tottering figure and half-dragged, half-carried her through the door of the ward. In the corridor outside he clamped his palms against her shoulders and pinned her to the wall, holding her upright by sheer force. Earnestly he spoke into the averted face.

'You can't faint here! Miss—wake up! Steady the Buffs—fall in there—now, then! There's a good lass!'

For a minute he thought she had lost her senses completely and braced himself to catch her before she hit the floor. But the blue-veined lids flickered, and her dazed eyes slowly opened, seeming to stare through him. Valiantly she pressed her palms on the wall behind her, and forced herself erect. She drew a shivering breath.

'Good girl! That's right—breathe deep now! You'll be better in a minute!'

'Please . . . tell me—'

Her voice failed. She tried again.

'Grindle—please—I still do not quite . . .'

'Major Melrose and Mr Verrall,' reiterated Grindle, with kindly patience. 'Escaped from the Russian jail—came back by sea—God knows how! Major Melrose is at Headquarters; Mr Verrall here at the hospital!'

Her head fell back against the wall; her lids closed. Her face was whiter than the cap she wore. Slowly, her lips moved.

'*Dear God in heaven*,' breathed Tess.

Even as Grindle moved to catch her, he saw in

astonishment a remarkable change take place. The cornflower eyes of Nurse Mainwaring flew suddenly wide open, and shone straight into his own with a light that grew, and grew—like the stars, thought Grindle; he had never seen anything to match it! As he watched, her cheeks turned warm and rosy—red lips parted—teeth glimmered like pearls . . . She seemed to grow in stature; the white neck arched, and the golden head lifted—and the pale girl who a minute past had drooped before him like a wilting lily now stood, alive, glowing, pulsing with health and eagerness.

Grindle could only gape at her.

'Do you mean that he is *here*? Safe—well? *In this very hospital?*'

Grindle nodded, mute.

She snatched at his rough old hands and cried out passionately, 'I must go to him! Now! This minute!'

'Hush—hush, lassie! You'll wake up the—'

She lowered her tone to a fierce whisper.

'Tell me where he is—tell me instantly!'

'He'll be in his quarters, I s'pose; that is—if he has finished making his report.'

'I have to see him! I must!'

She was clinging to his hands. The little man squeezed the shaking fingers in his own.

'Look,' he said, gently. 'Just calm down—just take it easy for a minute.' He glanced at her shrewdly, pursing up his wrinkled lids. 'I gather that you want to see this young feller pretty bad—'

'Yes—oh, yes!'

'But you'd like, wouldn't you, to see him alone? No one to listen in on you, eh?'

'Oh—! Oh, yes, I should . . . I—I had not thought . . .'

'Reckon you hadn't. Now . . . lemme see.' Grindle ruminated. She watched his face with painful attention. 'Mmm . . .' His grizzled brows settled over his nose. 'There's a place I know of—used to be a storeroom. Should be safe enough.' He came to a decision, smiling into her eyes. 'I reckon I can fix it. Now, I tell you what—'

'Yes?'

'You finish your duty here. Only a half-hour, ain't it? Not very long. You go back in there and finish off; we don't want to cause no fuss and bother, do we? Meantime, I'll go along and find this lad of yours. I'll tell him there's someone who wants to speak to him urgent, no names, no pack drill. When you come off here, I'll take you to him. And—just to be on the safe side—I'll stand guard meself outside the door, so as you're not disturbed.' He paused triumphantly. 'There! How's that?'

Tess gave a little cry and threw her arms around him. She hugged his thin body and kissed his leathery cheek.

'Dear Grindle!' She patted his face, smiling

tremulously. 'So very good—so very kind! Thank you!'

She turned about and whisked herself back within the ward. Grindle put a hand to the place where her lips had rested. A delighted grin split his face from ear to ear, and he wagged his head energetically, several times in succession. Still beaming and nodding he stumped off down the passage and proceeded to set a course for the surgeons' quarters.

The night was very beautiful. There was no moon, but it was scarcely needed, so brightly did the white stars of the Crimea light up the rich infinity of the deep blue sky.

Finger to lip, Grindle beckoned. Tess, casting a wary look into the shadows, followed obediently, wrapping her cloak tightly about her as they picked their way along the path. Everything seemed asleep. The night wind scattered a leaf here and there, but that was all. The various outbuildings that surrounded the main structure of the hospital lay behind them, darkened and quiet.

At last, Grindle spoke in a whisper, close beside her.

'Here we are, miss.'

They had reached the entrance. She touched his arm in thanks; he melted into the darkness.

The door swung inwards . . . She stepped across the threshold.

It was a small sordid room, musty and gloomy, with a single unglazed window. A few empty packing-cases stood about. On one of these, a candlestick had been placed.

Tess noticed none of these things. She saw only the young man who was standing by the window.

He was of medium height and powerfully made, though so gaunt and spare of frame that the army tunic swung loose from his flat shoulders. The candle-flame illumined straight brown hair, a young eagle face; the hand that rested on the window frame was lean and sensitive, and very strong.

Tess saw the outline of a stubborn jaw, a muscled throat; and even from there, across the width of the room in the dim light, she saw the eyes that were like no others she had ever seen; grey as glass, clear as spring-water; eyes with a clarity that could look, when he chose, into one's secret soul—and strip it bare, and leave it shivering.

She began to shake like a blown leaf.

Her hands fluttered; she made a hoarse sound, deep in her chest . . . Then she ran across the room into his arms.

They opened wide; they closed about her.

She lay on his breast, drowned in wonderment. His heart thudded against her own. Her head fell on his shoulder; little cries, that trembled into sobs, came from her, and over and over she said his name—as if repeating a charm that would keep him with her, real, alive and warm . . . until they grew old and died, and beyond that.

She heard his voice; the soft slurred voice with the gentle cadence of the west country that had bred him . . . against her face, against her hair, broken, incoherent.

'My dearest love . . . my only love—I never hoped—never dreamed—'

Touching his lips, caressing his face, she brushed aside the heavy hair from his forehead. Her fingertips found the jagged line of the scar that ran from above his eyebrow, across and down over the cheekbone. She moaned.

'You are hurt . . . You have suffered—pain, and cold, and hunger . . . all these long months past! And I did not know . . . Oh! My love, my love—!'

Her flesh cried out for him. She clung to him and whirled away from the dark room, past the trees and the stars, to some place where there was sun and light and flowers. She twined her arms around his neck, arching her back, and raised her mouth to his; fiercely, his arms tightened; she felt the fire in his blood, the ardent flare of passion in him—her veins danced and tingled.

A little breeze puffed in through the window and flickered the candle-flame. Somewhere in the dark outside a night bird was crying gently.

'You are safe—*safe*!' She was laughing and crying together; her cheeks were glowing, yet wet with tears. 'It's true—true—you are here! Alive . . . Oh, love!' She lifted luminous eyes. 'We shall go home—together! And—and we shall be married.'

Suddenly it was all too much for her.

Overwhelmed, she sank against him. Streaks of blackness shot past her eyes—the floor heaved under her feet.

Roger caught her up in strong arms, lifting her high against his breast. There was no place to lay her down in that rough room. He carried her to an upturned case and eased her gently on to it; he held her close, caressing the bright head, cradling her on his chest like a child. By degrees, she ceased to shiver and began to grow calm, soothed by his touch, his voice, the incredible warm reality of his nearness. Her dizziness faded and was succeeded by a delicious, dreamy quiescence.

Tranquil, in absolute contentment, they sat together on the packing-case. His arm was about her; her hand clasped in his.

There was nothing more for either of them to need, or to know.

It was Roger who came back first, slowly, drawn back into the reality of the dark dirty room, the place, the night outside and around them. He blinked at the candle; the small flame seemed to dazzle him; his grey eyes stared blindly at it. His gaze turned to the girl who lay in his arms. Her face was averted, nestled in his shoulder; her eyes were closed—the lashes like rays of darkness on the satiny cheeks. A little smile played about her mouth. She leaned on him, her body relaxed—utterly childlike, defenceless.

The face of Roger Verrall changed. Suddenly, it fell into taut-drawn lines, as if the bones were closer to the surface, stretching the skin. A deep groove settled from nose to mouth, the nostrils grew waxen; he looked, in that moment, worn and weary, and older than his twenty-six years.

'Tess . . . I must talk to you.'

She smiled more deeply, and moved her head closer into the hard hollow between his throat and shoulder. She said in a drowsy murmur,

'So happy, love . . .'

He raised his head and took a slow breath. Very carefully he disengaged his hand from hers, and withdrew his supporting arm. Then he rose to his feet and faced her.

'No—stay there.' He stopped her with a gesture, as she made to come to him. 'Tess! There's no help for it!' The moving light glimmered in his eyes. 'There is something I must say . . . And it must be said now.'

There was an intensity about him that began to puzzle her.

'When I was told that someone wished to speak to me—'

He stopped abruptly. She waited.

'I offer no excuses for my conduct, for there can be none . . . My lady, you must return to the hospital—immediately!'

Bewilderment gave way to glad comprehension. She jumped to her feet.

'Now I understand! You are concerned for my reputation!' She laughed. 'Why—that is thoughtful, sir; but if I should be seen—I do not care! We are betrothed!'

He walked to the window, and stood with his back to the room, looking out. His knuckles were white on the frame.

'You don't understand.' It was a sort of groan. 'Listen to me, Tess! We are not betrothed. We can never be.'

The words fell heavily into a sudden silence. The candle-flame sent shadows moving on the wall.

At last, Tess moved jerkily forward; she came to the window as if pulled by strings. One hand touched his arm. He made no response. His profile looked stern. She searched it, anxious, disbelieving; the closed face was empty of expression, the eyes withdrawn, half-hooded. Her hand stole to his shoulder. Huskily, she asked,

'Roger—what is wrong? What is the matter?'

He turned his head and looked full into her eyes.

'It isn't possible. It never was. Tess—you and I—must not meet again.'

She gasped aloud. His eyes, fringed with start-ling black, bored into her—fixed and suspended her. They held something pitiless, like a naked sword. Shock, and a kind of fear, grew within her, and spread, turning her cold. She could only stand before him, without volition. Her mouth framed some words, but none came.

'I am no husband for you . . . I wish that you might have been spared this! I believed you to be far away in England. When I saw you there—in that doorway . . . I—' He faltered; there was a pause. When he spoke again, the tone was flat, his voice held a ruthless finality. 'We are not engaged, and we never were. That is the end of the matter.'

All the soft and lovely colour drained from her face. At last, from somewhere a long way off, her words came, through lips that were stiff and wooden.

'You—you do not love me?'

He turned away from her, and said, between his teeth, 'I do not.'

She twisted her hands to stop their shaking. There was a ringing in her ears. But she said in a voice that did not waver,

'Roger! You must look at me—and say so. then . . . I will believe it.'

There was no reply. The seconds ticked away.

Tess cried out then, with a throb of anger,

'You are lying! I knew it! But why? Why should you? I don't understand!'

'I think,' he answered evenly, 'that you understand well enough.'

A tinge of red ran into Tess's white cheeks. The icy numbness within her began to melt before a swell of temper. Her eyes sparked, and the angry flush deepened as she looked at him through narrowed lids.

In the same controlled tone, Roger added, 'There is nothing more to be discussed. Return to the hospital now.'

She suddenly flared.

'Nothing to be discussed! Is that so, indeed! You are damned high-handed! I won't be dismissed so!'

As though she had not spoken, he repeated steadily, 'You must go back now.'

'Don't order me away like a naughty child! I shan't go! I shall stay here until you explain!'

'I have done so. You are free of your engagement.'

'Oh—!' With storm signals flying, Tess panted, 'You break your promise, then! You are dishonourable, Roger Verrall!'

His eyes flashed with a sudden fire that matched her own.

'If you say so, Lady Eustacia!'

'Don't address me so!'

'I'll address you as I choose!'

They glared at each other in snapping silence. The air crackled between them.

With lips compressed, Roger turned away.

There was an electric pause. At last, he made an abrupt gesture and brought his gaze back to her face; his eyes softened, his mouth lost its grim line.

He stepped to her, and took both her hands in a firm, strong grasp.

'Tess. Please . . . you must listen. When we first met in England, that first morning, you shone like a light in that poor room—you . . . the loveliest thing I had ever seen or dreamed of— But then—I did not know—'

She broke in.

'Yes, yes! I deceived you—I lied! I meant to tell you the truth. I would have done so! You must know that—And now—it makes no difference—no difference at all!'

'If, at that time,' he went on quietly, 'I had been aware of your identity, of the name you bear, I never would have spoken. Tess—you must understand—you have not thought! You— a lady of rank, a great heiress—and I—'

'Yes?' Head high, flags flying, she challenged him. 'Yes—and you?'

'Your commonsense must make it plain! A farmer's son—an obscure surgeon, without birth or fortune. Such a match is out of the question— impossible.'

She answered, choking, 'I might have thought that *I* would be allowed some say in that!'

He said deliberately, 'On the contrary, my lady. You have no say whatsoever.'

She gasped, and flung up her chin. He gripped her hands.

'You are as you were born, Tess. You will return to England—take your proper place—'

She tried to pull free from his grasp. He felt the roughened tips of the slim white fingers, and the abraded patches on the smooth skin. His heart turned over.

Angrily, he burst out, 'It isn't right—you ought not to be here at all! This work—it's not fit for you!'

Tess tore her hands from his, and flung away from him, with heaving breast. Born of the long months of sadness and pain, of weariness and overtaxed strength, a tide of hot and bitter words rose in her throat and overflowed on her tongue.

She hurled them at him.

'So that is it—that is what you really think of me! A—a useless doll—unfit to nurse! Unfit for anything, in your eyes!' She whirled, and began to pace the room, laughing wildly. 'You *fool*! Do you know what I have done—what I have *seen*?' Her voice rose shrilly. 'This is intolerable! I won't have it!'

She came to a halt, and confronted him with glittering eyes. Her voice fell to a sibilant hiss.

'You stand there—so cold, so sure—but now I see the truth! Oh, yes—now I see it . . .' She spat the words. 'You are false—were always so! From the beginning you were false!'

Roger turned white round the mouth.

He took one furious stride, and grabbed her by the elbows.

'*False!*' His fingers bit into her arms. 'False—when I would give my life, my soul—' She quailed before the blaze at the back of his eyes. 'By God! You shall not dare to say so!'

In all her life she had never been so used.

Seized, shaken, crushed, she was helpless against his iron chest; her ribs were breaking, she could not breathe. His fierce mouth, burning and relentless, was clamped to her own. Her feet seemed to leave the floor—her head was swimming.

When he released her at last, she tottered, staring, a hand to her bruised mouth. The flesh of her arms throbbed from his ruthless fingers; her lips were hot and swollen; she felt scorched all over.

Roger strode to the door and threw it wide. His eyes were gleaming slits.

'Go!' His face was inexorable. 'Do as I tell you!'

The Lady Eustacia drew herself upright.

With quaking knees, and nose elevated to its utmost, she marched past him through the doorway. She did not look back.

Standing outside, patient and forgotten, Grindle detached a shoulder from the wall. He shot a curious glance at the face of the young officer framed in the aperture, and thence at the retreating back of the lady whose erect carriage and haughty mien were slightly offset by a dangling loop of loosened gold descending over one ear. Grindle creased up his mouth, and gave a soundless whistle as he scurried after her rapidly diminishing form. He caught her up and followed at a respectful distance, keeping a pace or two in the rear.

Roger watched the two figures out of sight. Then he turned back into the room and crossed rather wearily to the window. Leaning his head on the frame, he stood looking into the night; the candle guttered and flickered. It had burned down almost to a stump when at last he quitted the room and made his way back through the dark to the surgeons' quarters.

CHAPTER
EIGHT

TESS SAT on a green grassy bank and gazed out at the shifting waters of Balaclava Bay. The sun warmed her, and the blue sky arched wide above her. Her hair, free for once from the confining cap, lay in a loose curly knot on her neck. She shook back the soft mass of it, lifting her face to the light, feeling the wind on her cheeks; a bird swooped away into the glassy heights, and she watched it with eyes narrowed against the dazzle.

Her grey skirt fanned out over the short crisp turf. A pale flower poked through the grass; she nipped it off, turning it idly in her fingers. Loves me, loves me not . . .

'Dammit!' ejaculated Tess through small white teeth. 'I know he loves me! Wretch!'

She pitched the luckless flowers into the middle distance and sat brooding, chin on hands, eyes fixed on the place where sea and sky met. She wished, rather forlornly, that Rachel could be sitting here beside her. Without being specific, of course, she could have explained to Rachel in a very satisfactory fashion the sheer

stubbornness, the amazing stupidity and the unbelievable perversity of disposition exhibited in
general by the male sex.

'How dare he look at me so!' fumed Tess. 'For
two whole weeks . . . to be so distant, so—so
courteous! It's not to be borne!'

Her mouth had begun to tremble, and she bit
her lip; for if the precious anger and resentment
that buoyed her up were allowed to cool, it
would be superseded—as she knew too well—by
a sadness that was like a physical pain.

'I won't cry, I won't . . . I—I hate him!'

Her need of him was simple and profound. His
presence fired her blood and tingled every nerve,
but beyond that, transcending it, was a deep
instinctive comprehension of a tough energy in
him—a sort of power, a vitality, which she could
meet, and match, and absorb; becoming, with
him, a new substance, strong and bright, in a
brighter, intenser world. She sensed it, she knew
it, and—she reflected bitterly—he knew it too
. . . Only—he was Roger Verrall; more un-
reasonable, more obstinate, more arrogant than
any man she had ever—

Nurse Mainwaring ground her teeth with
some fervour. She glowered at the prospect
spread out before her, and blinked to dispel an
ominous prickling behind her eyes.

She picked another flower and cupped it in her
hand, tracing its outlines with a forefinger; she
held it up against the light, squinting at the

transparent petals in the dazzle of the water. Her shoulders were hunched, and her mouth and jaw wore a stubborn set which her old nurse at Ribston would instantly have recognised, had she seen it.

He is mine, thought Tess. Mine. I shall have him for my husband—I, and no other.

The fact that in the world's eyes it would be an unequal match, a *mésalliance*, did not register with her. Her brother Justin, on the night when he had brought her home from the tenement room where she had gone to see Roger for the last time, had said various unkind things to her; she had told him, on that occasion, that the words of small stupid people meant nothing to her. It was the simple truth. She had never, in her life, given a second thought to the opinions of such persons. It did not occur to her to do so now.

Her sister Lucy had known of her love for the young surgeon whom she had met by so strange a chance, and Lucy had helped her, for love was something that Lucy could comprehend very well indeed—so radiantly, so gloriously happy as she was with her new husband! But even Lucy could not understand what she saw as the sacrifice of Tess's life, after they had wept over the casualty list, after Roger was lost . . . for then, Lucy could not forbear to point out that Lord Weatherall and a brilliant marriage were awaiting the crook of a finger, and that all the luxuries and elegancies and pleasures of life were still to be enjoyed . . . No, even dearest Lucy had been nonplussed by Tess's determination to whistle it all down the wind—could not grasp that such things seemed useless, and pointless, and empty . . . That it was necessary for one to do something that was *real* . . .

I am glad I have money, mused Tess, for it will be put to good use and will certainly not lie idle. Certain plans, as yet unformulated, chased themselves around in her head. And Roger . . . so gifted he is, so skilled—to what heights may he not rise in his chosen profession? Watching him about the hospital she had been reminded, even more forcibly, of what she had known from the first; that he was kind, and clever, and strong with an inner strength that seemed to communicate itself to his patients; she saw that they trusted him, and looked for his coming, and were the better for it. She thought, gladly, that the money might help him in his work. Oh, yes! It is very fortunate!

Tess lifted her arms, stretching her back, and tucked the flower behind her ear. Her sadness and bewilderment had ebbed away; a sort of tranquillity took hold of her. Why, he is alive, and we love each other; nothing matters but that! And I am a nurse, and have seen what he has seen, and worked as he has done—we are fit, each for the other! He must see that— he shall see it; he has not, as yet, had sufficient time to think; that is all . . .

The footsteps that approached behind her were noiseless on the springy turf. She heard nothing, and looked up sharply as a shadow fell between her and the sun.

A momentary bright hope lit up her eyes—and as quickly faded.

Against the blue she saw scarlet, and glinting gold and polished leather; a cold high-nosed visage, black eyes, and under the waxed moustache a full-lipped red mouth that bore an ingratiating smile.

'How d'ye do, Lady Eustacia?' The brilliant apparition executed a graceful bow. 'Travis Hemrick, ma'am, at your service.'

In a single supple movement Tess sprang to her feet.

Hemrick offered his arm with a flourish.

'Will you do me the honour of walking with me, ma'am?'

He encountered a frosty stare from the lady's eyes.

Tess drew her cloak about her as though drawing away from something noxious, and turned to leave him.

He caught at a grey fold as it swished by him.

'Lady Eustacia! Wait—please!'

She spoke with icy hauteur.

'Kindly release me.'

He was anxious, placating.

'Won't you allow me to apologise—most

humbly—for my behaviour at Scutari? I want to assure you of my contrition—my deep regret—'

She flicked him over with glacial contempt.

'You are detaining me, sir.'

'May I not be your friend? I am acquainted with your brother, you know.'

She looked past him.

'It is the truth,' Hemrick persisted. 'We were at school together. Justin Mainwaring—I know him well. Please listen to me—let me explain—'

'I am quite indifferent to anything you may have to say.' Tess twitched her cloak away and spun on her heel.

'I only wish to be your devoted friend and servant,' Hemrick said urgently, to her back. 'Can you not bring yourself to forgive me?'

Tess sighed wearily.

'Sir, I find you tedious. Good-day to you.' She swung away, leaving him standing.

By the time she had reached the shelter of the hospital building she had dismissed him from her mind.

Coming off duty the following day, walking into the dormitory, Tess stopped short.

'What's this!'

A little bustling nurse, rather pink in the face, said breathlessly,

'Oh, Tess! My hair—could you—?'

'There you are, Mary.' Tess twisted up the refractory plait and skewered the cap to it. 'Who has brought these flowers?'

'I didn't see. There's a card, I think,' answered the little nurse, and departed post-haste.

Tess's bed was half obscured by a giant bouquet of roses. They were superb, and carefully wrapped in silver tissue with a silver-edged card attached.

Tess picked up the card and read the inscription.

'From your humble friend and respectful admirer.'

She made a face, and tore the card in two. Gathering up the roses she went in search of Mrs Thiele, and was fortunate to encounter that lady in the hall outside Miss Nightingale's room.

'Could these be placed in one of the wards, ma'am?'

Mrs Thiele took the gigantic bunch and sniffed it with pleasure.

'Flowers in a military ward . . .' She mused. 'Indeed—why not? They are lovely—and sufficient to furnish several wards, I should think!' She smiled at the girl. 'Come with me, nurse, we shall see if there are any vases to be found.'

The door to Miss Nightingale's room stood ajar. As they went by, Tess caught a glimpse of the dark-clad figure seated upright at the desk. The sun was shining outside, but a lamp burned near the absorbed face, and the thin hand propping her forehead looked transparent in its rays. Even in that brief moment Tess observed the pallor that lay over the intent features, and the grey shadows about the mouth.

Mrs Thiele followed her glance. She made a tiny sound of exasperation.

'All night in the wards,' she breathed, as they moved softly away, 'and now she will not sleep! I have tried to persuade her—but she won't listen. I don't know what to do with her!'

Tess lay tossing in her cot, between sleeping and waking. The night seemed abnormally warm and oppressive. Restlessness plagued her, as the slow hours passed; fitful periods of unconsciousness alternated with vague and jumbled dreams; she was walking with Roger in a green meadow, but he drew away from her, and vanished; she jolted into wakefulness, and turned her hot pillow and thumped it soundly. The air in the dormitory seemed stifling to her in spite of the open windows, and when at last the dawn broke, it was dull and grey, with no freshness in the air.

It was a rather heavy-headed nurse who rose from her bed as the light filtered into the room. Pulling on the thick black stockings, fastening the heavy worsted jacket, she thought with wistfulness of muslin, and perhaps a fetching hat of delicate straw with satin ribbons down her back, mingling with her curls. She leaned forward to the mirror as she fastened her cap, and studied the features in the glass . . . Staring at the reflected face, she pictured it framed in shining ringlets twined with rosebuds and pearls; a dress of silk, with lace and flounces—the frou-frou of rustling petticoats . . . He has never seen me so, she thought; and sighed. It was almost eight o'clock. She gave a final glance in the mirror, a last tug to the jacket, and departed in the direction of the ward.

Immediately she was swept into the routine of the day. Sweat-soaked bodies to be washed and clothed in fresh linen; beds to be made, broth carefully spooned into slackened mouths, wounds dressed, bandages changed—the busy hours went by. The long ward seemed gloomy, and the air thick, as low clouds continued to obscure the sun. Tess's hands worked on; but a certain feeling of detachment which had beset her since opening her eyes remained to plague her, resisting her efforts to shake it off.

Mrs Thiele beckoned.

'When you have finished that dressing, fetch writing materials here. This man wishes to send a message to his home. He is too weak to hold a pen, but can dictate the words to you, nurse.'

Tess obediently procured ink, pen and paper and seated herself beside the soldier, with writing tablet balanced on her knee. In a low voice, the man began to speak; she had transcribed the words, 'Dearest Mother—I am in the hospital at Balaclava—', when the voice faltered and stopped. With pen poised, Tess looked at him; he had a thin, intelligent countenance, with rather large dark eyes. She waited; no more was forthcoming. She passed a hand across her forehead, which felt as if it were wearing an iron band, and asked,

'What would you like to say?'

The soldier said faintly, 'It's no use. I can't—'

'What is the matter? Are you in pain?'

He turned his head away from her and gave a crack of empty, mirthless laughter.

'Pain! No—I feel nothing!'

'Then what—?'

'My mother, my father . . . I don't know them—don't know what to say to them. They are strangers to me now. I—am not the son that they knew—'

Tess said briskly, 'Of course you are! Why, your wounds are healing perfectly. You will be well again quite soon!'

With a sort of quiet desperation, the man said,

'No—you don't understand. I look at blood, and hear my comrades suffer, and I don't see it, or hear it. I feel nothing—I am a dead man . . .' He lifted his head from the pillow. 'Empty—hollow—dead!'

Tess sat nonplussed. Her wits had deserted her; her brain would not function; the soldier's face was ashen and his gaze was fixed on her in a kind of dumb entreaty—his body was trembling violently. Clearly, he was on the point of a nervous collapse, and speech had fled from her. For once totally inadequate, her head filled with cotton wool, Tess sat mumchance. She cleared her throat, opened her mouth, and closed it again.

A voice spoke behind her. She started, and rose hastily to her feet.

Mrs Thiele said calmly to the soldier,

'There is no need for despair.' She moved forward, bent over the man and took his hands in her own. 'Not one of us,' went on the quiet, reassuring voice, 'not one, out of us all, is unchanged by what has happened here.'

The man gripped her hand. His eyes turned to the face above him.

'There is bitterness, and suffering, in life; and it comes to all,' went on the senior nurse. 'But our own true selves, deep within us, do not change—and can never do so.' With her free hand she straightened the pillow, and pressed him gently down. 'You have forgotten how to sleep, that is all; nothing more.' She touched his forehead; he looked up at her with unashamed tears. 'Rest, now; you are tired. When you awaken, nurse will write your letter for you.' Under her touch, his eyes fluttered, closed; he nodded, very faintly. She stood quietly watching him as he grew calm and relaxed; presently his breathing deepened. Mrs Thiele motioned Tess away from the bed, and said in an undertone,

'Poor lad; he is too highly strung. With a patient of that type, nurse, reassurance is important, and sleep is vital. Remember it, if you please.'

Without waiting for a reply, the senior nurse turned and went noiselessly away. With respect, and something that bordered on awe, Tess looked after her.

The clatter and bustle of the midday meal came and went; the ward settled to quiet again. Some walking wounded were brought in with minor injuries to be cleansed and dressed. There were attended to in a kind of annexe opening from one end of the room, on this particular day, the duty of out-patients fell to Tess.

A tall infantryman, quite young in years but with grey threads in his beard, stood quietly at the end of the line awaiting his turn. When Tess came to him at last he withdrew his hand from the breast of his tunic and held it out for her to see. She unwrapped the dirty rag and laid bare the hand. The palm was badly lacerated and inflamed. She made a little sound of concern and turned the hand over.

The wound on the back of the hand was much smaller, and almost symmetrical in shape. She looked, and under the crusted blood and dirt perceived the tell-tale dark stain of a powder-burn . . . a bullet-wound inflicted at close quarters.

Tess caught her breath. She stared at the man, and he stared back; she knew . . . and he sensed her knowledge. They were, for the moment, alone in the annexe. Tess shot a quick glance over her shoulder, through the open doorway into the ward. No one was looking in their direction.

It was her duty to report him. The penalty for self-inflicted wounds was harsh and summary. She brought her gaze back to him—the hand that she held was trembling . . . He stood mute, defenceless, before her. His shoulders sagged, and in his face she read a profound exhaustion, a weariness of mind and body beyond which it was no longer possible to endure. She risked another glance into the long room. Mrs Thiele was no longer there, having moved on at midday to another ward; Mary, her companion on duty, was occupied with a patient farther along; her profile was turned to Tess, and her face intent.

Basins, bandages and scissors were laid ready on a small table beside them. Tess moved slightly so that her body screened the patient, and began to work quickly. Her own hands were trembling a little, for if a surgeon should come in, or even an orderly, the game was up; the soldier's punishment would be sure—as for herself, she did not know; dismissal would probably be the least of it. Swiftly and deftly she washed the torn flesh, cleansed the jagged edges and drew them together as best she could, and wound the bandage about it. Bones grated in the back of the hand; she tried to straighten them while he stood in dumb stoicism, then swathed the hand well, for support. When it was done, she whispered, 'There . . . Say nothing. I think it will heal.'

His lips moved; then, with lowered head, he

turned away. As he walked out of the annexe, the head surgeon appeared. In his usual fussy manner, he snapped,

'What man is that, nurse? Who is he?'

'The last of the walking wounded, sir.' Tess's colour was slightly heightened, as she bent over the table and began to set it to rights.

'Oh! What was his injury?'

'A sabre cut, sir,' replied Tess, intent upon folding an unused arm-sling. Crockford glanced at her sharply—her face was expressionless. He sent his gaze travelling around the annexe, found nothing to complain of, and departed as fussily as he had come.

Tess exhaled a long noiseless breath of relief. Feeling rather limp, she restored the annexe to neatness, gathered up the surgical materials and returned to the ward. The headache which had been threatening to spring upon her since she had awakened in the sultry dawn now decided to wait no longer. Her temples began to throb, and continued to do so, with relentless and monotonous regularity, as the afternoon wore on.

It was just past three o'clock when the sergeant of Fusiliers was brought in. He came on his feet, with his arms dragging over the shoulders of the two orderlies who supported him, but it was plain that he was oblivious to what was happening about him. A bloodstained cloth was twisted round his head. When the makeshift dressing was removed, an ugly wound was revealed beneath the matted, clotted hair. He was a burly black-bearded man with heavy shoulders and broad chest; it took the united efforts of Tess, Mary and the two orderlies to strip away the tattered filthy uniform, sponge the feverish body and get him into clean nightshirt and clean bed. The cot nearest the door was vacant, and between them they settled him into it, although he was restless and struggled against their helping hands. Roger came in before the task was completed, and set about sponging the wounded head and trimming away the hair to lay the injury bare. His touch, and his quiet voice, seemed to soothe the patient; watching his strong deft hands skilfully stitching the wound, Tess murmured, half to herself,

'There is a fracture, I think . . .'

Roger glanced up at her, with sharp approval.

'You see it? Here—touch here—very gently. The bone is depressed slightly . . . He is concussed, of course.'

She felt the place with one forefinger, delicately, sensing the softness beneath; Roger watched closely; the two young faces were absorbed, concentrated upon the patient. 'Yes—there—I can feel it . . .'

The man began to stir and mutter. One great arm swung wildly; Tess caught it, and found that it took all her weight to bear it down on the mattress. Panting a little, she asked,

'Should we restrain him, do you think?'

Roger stood for a moment in thought.

'I dislike the practice,' he answered, at last. 'I believe that it harms a patient to be tied to a bed, no matter what the circumstances. I will post an orderly to watch beside him until he settles down of his own accord.'

He stepped back, nodded politely to both nurses, spoke a few words to the orderly, and departed. Tess restrained her eyes from following him.

The afternoon waned; beyond the windows a dull sunset sank into a clouded afterglow. Lamps were lit in the wards. Lounging beside the bed where the sergeant lay, an orderly whistled silently between his teeth. Another hour slipped by.

Tess looked round to find the orderly at her elbow.

'I'm going for my dinner, miss.'

She looked at him doubtfully.

'Shouldn't you ask the surgeon's permission?'

'Can't do that if he ain't here, can I?'

Tess moved along the ward and approached the bed where the sergeant lay.

'Hasn't stirred for an hour,' pointed out the orderly. 'Won't wake up until morning, I wouldn't be surprised.'

It was true enough; the patient lay quietly, his hands relaxed on his chest; his eyes were closed, his breathing heavy but regular.

'Sleeping like a baby,' urged the orderly. 'I

ain't had any dinner yet, miss.'

Tess touched the soldier's forehead; he did not stir. He gave every appearance of being sunk in profound sleep.

'I'm going, miss. Dead to the world, 'e is—'

Her head was pounding. With a little snap, she said,

'Very well—go, then! And you had better hurry back!'

The orderly gave her a cocksure grin, and took himself off.

Half an hour had gone by, with no sign of the orderly's return, when the sergeant who lay in the bed nearest the door raised himself on one elbow.

With a sort of angry desperation, he looked about him. The bandages about his skull reached almost to his eyebrows, and the eyes beneath were rimmed and suffused. They rolled around and turned from side to side, searching the room, travelling over the walls and the ceiling.

The sergeant shook his head, and blinked. His wavering gaze came to rest on the two grey figures along the ward. Darkness was drawing in, a few stars shining out in the sky past the windows; the shapes of the two nurses were outlined by lamplight. Both girls were intent upon a patient who was moaning and tossing; one of them was holding a lamp close to the bed. Their low voices came as an indistinct murmur of sound to the watcher at the far end.

The nurse Mary was saying, 'He is still very fevered . . .'

'That shoulder is bandaged too tight,' whispered Tess. 'Do you support him while I loosen it a little.'

The waving shadows of the two white-capped heads were thrown on the opposite wall.

In the end bed, the sergeant put a hand to his swathed head, jerked his limbs about, and suddenly sat bolt upright.

The girls' faces were turned from him; he saw their caps in a white blur. Keeping his eyes trained upon their backs, he swung his legs to the floor.

Standing up, he staggered a little and reached to steady himself on the wall. Crabwise, with arms outspread, he began to creep along it.

The two nurses laid the fevered man back on his pillow. Mary took a sponge and began wiping the flushed face.

'While you do that,' Tess murmured in her ear, 'I will see to the others.'

The groping fingers of the sergeant stretched to the doorjamb. He pushed the door ajar, and slipped through.

Tess took up the tiny lamp and began to move from bed to bed, pausing here and there to bend over the occupant. At last she reached the cot that was nearest the door.

For a second she stood staring, dumbfounded. The covers had fallen to the floor. She saw the door still ajar, and darted to the entrance, peering along the corridor. The twilight was fading, and in the gathering gloom, she could see no sign of the injured man.

'Good God—!'

White-faced, Mary quavered, 'Whatever shall we do?'

Trying to steady her trembling voice, Tess said bravely,

'Surely he can't have gone far! If—if only he has not got out of the building! Mary, can you take charge here? I will run and look for him, and raise the alarm!'

Mary nodded.

Outside the door, Tess hesitated for a moment, and then sped away to the nearest angle of the hall. From here the passage led in virtually a straight line as far as the outer door of the hospital.

Measuring the distance from where she stood, Tess concluded that it was too far. The man could not have traversed it in so short a time. She turned about and began to race in the opposite direction. Rounding a bend, full tilt, she encountered the orderly returning. She gasped,

'Tell the surgeons—Miss Nightingale! The sergeant—escaped—wandering in the hospital!' She dodged past him and continued running, leaving him gaping.

Faster and faster she went, sending her eyes in every direction, down every length of hall. She could discern nothing anywhere that was out of the ordinary, and began to grow afraid.

Suddenly, however, she picked up the faint echo of some sort of commotion. She strained her ears and heard what seemed to be the sound of a distant shout.

The noise grew louder. A second far-off yell followed the first.

Tess's heart began to pound. She had located the source of the disturbance; it was coming from the direction of the kitchens. She increased her speed; her stout shoes skidded on the uncovered slippery floor as she picked up her skirts and flew round the corners. As she drew closer, the sounds of confusion became more imperative.

She reached the main door of the kitchen and burst in.

It was the hour of the evening meal, and the large room was crowded. The tables were covered with food and utensils. Various excited persons were milling about, gesticulating, offering advice; they stumbled, and got in one another's way. Some of the cookhands stood at their benches, transfixed, their chopping-knives halfway to the blocks. The place was full of urgent voices, exclaiming and exhorting, and across the room near the far wall, a vociferous group was talking loudly and pointing at someone standing near one of the fireplaces.

Tess pushed her way through the press of bodies.

The sergeant was backed up against the brick wall. He stood in the shallow refuge between wall and hearth. His head was thrust forward, under lowered brows. His chin wobbled as he weaved his face from side to side, and his eyes were glassy, in the leaping light of the flames. His open mouth was a moving black hole from which poured forth a jumbled stream of incoherent syllables.

In his hand was a long butchering-knife. He had snatched it up from a table and held it before him. The knife was broad and razor-sharp; firelight danced merrily along the edge of the blade.

Tess started to say, 'Don't be afraid—'

One of the kitchenhands, more bold or foolhardy than his fellows, suddenly leaped from the group of onlookers. He flung himself at the man with the knife.

Tess shrieked, 'Don't! You mustn't—'

The knife slashed wickedly. The kitchenhand lurched back and fetched up against a table. The watching faces swivelled towards him, and a sort of sigh went up. He put a hand to his forearm, and blood dripped between the fingers.

Dismay and altercation rose to the ceiling.

Through the clamour, Tess shouted, 'Grip your arm tight—I'll attend to you directly! But you should not have done that!'

There was a stir at the kitchen door. A number of persons bustled in. Mr Crockford was in the lead, Roger was at his heels.

'What's this—what's this?' fretted the chief surgeon. His prominent eyes took in the scene. 'Here!' he barked. 'Don't stand about! Some of you men bunch together, and rush him! Get in under his guard!'

There was a concerted movement. Fists were clenched—one of the bolder spirits picked up a fire-iron and brandished it over his head.

'Now!' cried Mr Crockford.

'Wait!' Roger brushed the chief surgeon aside. 'All of you—wait.'

There was no heat in his voice, but somehow it carried a quality that cut through the din. Heads turned in his direction—by degrees, movement stilled.

Afterwards, those who stopped and stood, and listened to him, could not have said just why they had done so.

Roger waited quietly for the general confabulation to die away.

Then, unhurriedly, he strolled towards the fireplace. He came level with Tess; and almost absently, without removing his gaze from the man with the knife, he hooked an arm around her waist and stood her to one side, where she was shielded by the angle of a tall cupboard. He approached the man, still holding him with a steady regard, and halted a few feet away under the silent stares of the watchers.

The soldier returned his gaze. Sweat gleamed on the sergeant's face. The knife swept before him in a whistling half-circle.

A pause ensued. In the hush, somebody stumbled against a chair. The clatter and scrape split the silence, and the soldier started nervously. His eyes rolled and bulged, and the blade flicked like a striking snake.

Roger swore soundlessly.

He said through his teeth, 'Keep still . . . You lot near the fireplace, move back. No noise.'

Once again he was obeyed. Cautiously, those near the patient fell back, and so withdrew their round eyes and gaping mouths from his line of vision.

Roger and the soldier continued to contemplate each other.

From beside the cupboard, eyes peering, Tess saw Roger strangely in detail, as if magnified by a glass in her mind. He stood relaxed, almost negligent, one hand on hip, with an easy and confident carriage of his head. From where she was, she could not possibly have discerned the sickle-shaped scar under the brown hair that fell over his temple, or the gleam of golden down on a smooth cheekbone, or the tiny muscle that twitched the sensitive corner of his mouth; yet she saw all these things, nevertheless, with an awareness that encompassed his every slight movement, the breath that he drew, each separate bone in his body.

Roger took a pace forward. A ghastly sickness rose in Tess's mouth as she saw that the knife was within stabbing distance of his chest, his throat. He did not appear to notice; she opened her mouth to cry a warning—and shut it again, slowly.

When Roger spoke, he sounded cheerful.

'Sergeant. Your orders are to rest.'

The seconds ticked by.

Straining forward, poised on the balls of her feet, Tess watched the flickering knife-blade. The only chance of saving him, she decided, was to spring at the arm which held the weapon and throw all her weight upon it. With eyes painfully fixed on the glittering steel, she stirred, moved, as noiseless as a wraith, and began to steal forward.

Roger said, with laconic unconcern, 'The men have fallen back. The orders are to rest.'

Deliberately, he stepped closer. The blade moved; Tess drew herself taut, and gathered her muscles to spring.

'You have your orders, Sergeant.'

It seemed as if the patient would stand, with working mouth and eyes on the surgeon's face, for ever.

Then—at last, still staring, the soldier nodded his head, very slowly . . . once, twice.

He drew himself erect; his slack lips firmed. The hand that held the knife sketched the vestige of a salute, then relaxed and fell to his side.

Quietly, Roger reached out and removed the hilt from the unresisting fingers.

The patient put a hand to the wall to steady himself and watched, docile, as Roger reached high, placing the knife safely upon the mantelpiece.

Tess put a shaking hand to her head, and sagged against the cupboard. A slackening of tension, a sort of breath, sighed round the room among the watchers.

In that unguarded moment, the zealous youth who had armed himself with the fire-iron decided to make his bid for public acclaim.

Bounding forward, he brandished the iron bar and swung the weapon at the patient's bandaged skull.

Just in time Roger caught the upraised arm in a bone-crushing grip. The fire-iron fell to the hearth.

'Bloody fool!' snarled Roger.

He shook the hapless cookhand like a rat, and pitched him into the arms of the bystanders. The would-be hero slunk away and was lost in the crush.

Roger cast one quelling glance around the assembled company, and took the soldier by the arm.

'Come with me, Sergeant. I'll show you the way.'

A path cleared before them as they marched across the room. Nobody spoke as they departed.

Roger paid no attention to the presence of a tall thin lady in a dark dress who had arrived shortly after Mr Crockford's party, and who had watched the subsequent proceedings with interest. This lady looked closely into the face of the young surgeon as he passed by her, and the sharp eyes that rested thoughtfully upon his retreating figure held an enigmatic expression. She continued to look after the young man until both he and the patient were out of sight.

'Roger . . .' The whisper reached after him, and caught him on the threshold. Tess said, in a stifled undertone.

'I—I feel that the blame is mine.'

He glanced quickly towards the entrance of the ward. The annexe was empty; they were screened by the angle of the doorway. For a brief moment, they were alone.

He came to her.

'There is no blame—don't think that! These cases are unpredictable. I have set a watch on him for the rest of the night; you need not worry any more.'

She twisted her hands at her breast; her face was very white. She said, painfully,

'You—you could have been hurt . . .'

He caught the pathetic hands in his own; they were crushed in his grasp. She looked into his eyes. Motionless, hand-held, they stood together in the empty room. Her pale lips framed some words. Faintly, from far away, they came to him.

'I—can't bear this . . . Do you love me?'

There was a long moment of stillness. Approaching footsteps sounded within the adjoining ward.

He answered levelly, 'When I do not—there will be nothing left in this world.'

The footsteps came nearer; their hands fell apart . . .

In the dark hours of that night, Nurse Mainwaring lay huddled in her cot, burrowing down until only the top of a cornsilk head and the tip of a nose could be seen. The cheeks that resembled the tint and texture of Captain Hemrick's roses showed the glisten of tears, and yet a smile indented the corners of her mouth. She pulled the covers above her ears, crossed her arms on her breast, and hugged herself . . . Tightly holding in her love, and her pride in him, and the raw pain of her longing.

A little distance away, in another room, Miss Nightingale was seated at her desk. The journal before her was opened at a particular page. She sat and looked at it, considering it with care. 'This work, I find, makes of men either devils or angels . . .'

At last, she pulled the ink-bottle closer, and chose a pen. There was a short list of names inscribed upon the page; beneath a terse heading—'For Promotion'. She dipped the pen; and carefully, neatly, added another to the handful already there: 'Mr Verrall'.

CHAPTER
NINE

THROUGH THE days, and through the nights, the
'Frenchies' big guns' continued to pound at the
outermost fortification of Sebastopol—the huge
redoubt that was known as the Malakoff. Endless and deafening, the barrage went on. The
thunder and lightning of destruction roared and
flashed; the sky shrieked with it, the earth shuddered, the air sang with death. And still it went
on, for the Malakoff Redoubt was enormous,
awesomely fortified, seemingly impregnable;
but, unless it was taken, Sebastopol would not
fall.

And in the hospital at Balaclava, close behind
the lines, Miss Nightingale lay, helpless at last.

The body that had seemed not to need food, or
rest, or warmth, was—after all—only a human
body, with little strength left in it. It was as if a
tall tree or a high tower, which ought to have
remained standing unchanged and for ever, had
suddenly and incredibly crumbled and crashed
to the ground.

Waiting in the hall, as Mrs Thiele emerged
from the sickroom, Tess ventured,

'Please, ma'am—you must be so weary! Won't you take some rest? One of us could—'

Mrs Thiele spoke abstractedly.

'She has drunk a spoonful of the broth—Here, nurse, take the bowl. I think she may sleep a little. I must not stay.'

'If she is sleeping, won't you permit me to sit with her?'

'No, no—I shall not leave her.' Mrs Thiele turned back into the room. 'She looks for me. Even when she is wandering, she knows that I am by.'

The door closed behind her.

Days dragged past. Anxiety hung over the women like a cloud, and still the thin figure lay back against the pillows, too weak to lift its head.

Then July came in and brought the full warmth of summer. The bay lay sun-flecked and dimpling, the green deepened on the banks.

Perhaps it was the golden balm of the air that touched Florence Nightingale back to life or perhaps, somehow, the sound of the guns reached her, and reminded her that the work was not yet done. But a morning came, at last, when Mrs Thiele tiptoed from the sickroom, smiling.

The depleted body fought its way back, compelled as always by the mind that commanded it. She would never be strong again. It was a very frail and grey-faced lady who departed for Therapia to convalesce there where the hyacinth still bloomed, and bright vines sprang from the earth. Incredibly, however, her determination was such that before August was more than a few days old she was back in the Barrack at Scutari, to take the reins of management once more.

In the black of the nights, the Malakoff looked like a red erupting volcano under the bombardment of the allied guns. The French had almost four hundred, the British over one hundred, and from the sixth of June onwards, without respite, the assault on the Great Redoubt went on.

In the trenches the men waited, and wondered when the order would come to go over the top.

High up on the beetling redoubt, the Russian defenders were placed behind a fortification of five hundred guns. Sheltered by breastworks and dugouts, they answered the allied barrage bravely. When a gun was silenced, the Russian engineers worked grimly with skill and daring to get it firing again, while on the ramparts dapper young Russian officers paraded, resplendent in full dress uniform and white gloves—in defiance, and full view, of the enemy.

Within the fortified city, however, the carnage was fearful. 'The noise strikes the whole being,' wrote the young Count Tolstoy. 'It makes you shudder all over. A thick cloud of powder smoke envelops you—you are startled by the groans of a man covered with blood; half of his breast has been torn away . . .'

In Sebastopol's Orthodox Church the chant

for the dead wailed on night and day. The great ballroom, where young ladies had danced the night away after picnicking on the ramparts to watch the enemy perform their interesting manoeuvres, had been turned into a hospital. The parquet floor was covered in blood an inch deep.

And still the shells screamed, and exploded, and lit up the sky.

The day on which the Malakoff was to be stormed was set down, finally, for the eighteenth of June.

This was forty years—to the very day—since Lord Raglan, commander of the British, had lost an arm at Waterloo.

Now he was to lose his men.

Lord Raglan was very uneasy about this attack. True, the frightful cannonade from the allied guns had apparently silenced the defenders of the Malakoff at last. On the face of things, it seemed as an assault would meet almost no resistance. But, as the night hours ticked away and the hour of the dawn attack grew nearer, Lord Raglan's worry deepened.

He was a very old dog, and he knew of, and respected, the almost unbelievable ability of the Russian engineers to get their guns firing again, even in a few short hours. He had wanted—had asked for—the allied bombardment of the redoubt to continue through the night, until the very hour when his men went out to storm the walls. But the French commander had not thought it necessary, preferring to use the hours before daylight in massing his men for the assault. The allied guns were silent in the night, therefore, and up on the Malakoff, the Russians worked busily through the successive hours of darkness.

As the day broke, the refurbished Russian guns suddenly opened with terrible fire on the French soldiers assembled before the redoubt. The hail of death from the ramparts poured down on them; the range was almost point blank. No man could live in it.

Lord Raglan wanted to hold back his men, but to do so would mean breaking his word to his allies. To let the French down, at such a moment, was unthinkable.

Sick at heart, the old British warrior gave the order to go over the top—and sent his men into annihilation.

When the Royal Fusiliers leaped from the trenches, their colonel, sword in one hand and newfangled Colt revolver in the other, did not get five yards before he was riddled. The troops went headfirst into an awful confusion of smoke and shot. The Russian bullets were as big as apples; the outer barricade of the Malakoff was a shrieking hell of musketry, grape, canister and shell. The men went straight into it. In half an hour, eight thousand were lost.

Lord Raglan lived for twelve more days after that. The official cause of his death was given as cholera, but those who were closest to him knew better than that. The old man had sent his troops to destruction, and had died of a broken heart.

Mrs Thiele straightened her back, faltered, put a hand to her head.

'Are you not well, ma'am?'

'Perfectly.' Mrs Thiele steadied herself against the bedside table. 'A slight dizziness; nothing more. Now—concerning this patient—'

Tess opened her eyes.

The dormitory was still in darkness although the first paleness of dawn was in the sky. Puzzled, she lay and listened. Nothing disturbed the quiet of the room.

She was drifting back into another hour of precious sleep when the sound came again.

Instantly alert, she sat up in bed. There was no doubting, this time, as to what she had heard. It was a muffled groan, and it had come from somewhere close by.

Cloak shrugged on over her nightgown, she went barefooted to the door and tiptoed down the hall. She stopped outside a closed door; a series of choking gasps came from within. She pushed the door open.

'Mrs Thiele!'

The senior nurse was hunched up on the edge of her cot, doubled over, half in and half out of bed. She lifted a grey face as Tess ran to her.

'The cramps began at midnight. It's cholera,

I'm afraid.' Another spasm seized her. Through ashen lips, she whispered, 'Close the door, nurse . . . I am cold.'

With sinking heart Tess laid her palm on the other woman's forehead. She could feel the long uncontrollable tremors coursing through Mrs Thiele's body. She could also feel waves of heat rising under her hand; already the skin was fevered.

She put her arms about the shaking shoulders.

'Please, ma'am—you must lie down.'

Mrs Thiele started up in the bed.

'I cannot—must not!' she uttered. 'I have been placed in charge here . . . She trusted me! I have failed her—'

A convulsion gripped her entire frame. Shuddering before it, she fell back, gasping. Tess helped her on to the pillow.

'You have failed no one,' she declared, almost sternly. 'You must not think such a thing! Only rest now, I beg of you. Everything will go on—will be done—just as you wish! You may be sure!'

The ghost of a smile touched the pale corners of Mrs Thiele's mouth.

'On second thoughts . . . I am sure of it,' she gasped.

'Then, since you know that, dear ma'am, put your head on the pillow; close your eyes. I shall be gone for a minute only.'

Back in the dormitory, she bent over the

nearest bed and shook the occupant.

'Mary, Mary! It's Mrs Thiele—cholera!'

'Lord a'mercy—is she bad?'

'She seems so, at present—'

Mary was already out of bed.

'Go back to her, Tess. I'll bring all that is needed.'

'And Mary—some broth from the kitchen. Perhaps she might take some food before the fever rises—'

'Leave it to me,' said Mary, and departed at a run.

Lord Raglan was dead, and now the British found themselves playing second fiddle to the French commander. General Pélissier was an aggressive man, rough of speech and impatient. His refusal to acknowledge the skill of the Russians at repairing their guns in a hurry had made the attack on the Malakoff a costly failure. Too late, he realised it, and regretted it.

Pélissier knew, however, that the allied bombardment of the redoubt had caused heavy losses in the Russian fortress. His spies were competent, and the news they brought was pleasing. Within the walls of Sebastopol the dead were lying in piles; with every day that passed, more were dying of disease.

General Pélissier pondered on this gratifying intelligence. He came to the conclusion that there was no need to take the fortress by storm.

With the shrewdness of his Norman peasant ancestors, he realised that it was only necessary to sit and wait. When asked by his staff officers why the attempts to force an entry to Sebastopol did not continue, his explanation was simple. 'They are losing four hundred men a day. If we wait a month, they will have lost a division.'

Unfortunately, this prudence and caution did not suit the General's master, Louis Napoleon of France. Louis Napoleon dreamed of great conquests . . . (these were fought by soldiers, but the glory belonged to princes). Louis Napoleon was fresh from a visit to England, where the heady cheers of the admiring British, as he drove out to Windsor, still rang intoxicatingly in his ears. The personal honour accorded to him for the bravery of the French in battle was immensely exciting. He would have liked, in fact, to hurry out to the Crimea and take over the campaign himself; but the strategists, even in their state of temporary euphoria, could not stomach that.

Still, the picture was clear enough. Emperor Napoleon III had set his heart upon a victory that he could wear, like an extra jewel around his neck . . . So must it be.

Deeds of battle must resound; Sebastopol must fall—in a blaze of glory.

General Pélissier argued, and explained, and dug in his toes against the adjurations of his royal master. The Russians, watching, waiting, began to think that, after all, one last chance might be theirs.

If—in one last, all-or-nothing gamble—they were to move outside the city walls? They might, just might, be able to rush the invaders; fling them back—and drive them, once and for all, into the sea.

Word came presently to General Pélissier that the Russians were stirring, moving—massing men, guns, horses—in the hills outside the fort. The death or glory battle so ardently desired by Louis Napoleon was to take place after all, but there was little glory in it for anyone.

It was just dawn on the sixteenth of August when the Russians hurled themselves at the allied forces. It was ten o'clock, on the same morning, when they retreated, to take refuge within the fortress again. Twenty-three thousand soldiers lay dead upon the battlefield.

That was the signal to take Sebastopol. As the Russians fell back, the fire from the allied guns roared after them. It kept on roaring, blindly and madly, through the following dawns and the twilights. On the bastions above, gallant Russian gunners were chopped to pieces; others took their places—bravely, grimly—in the noise and the choking smoke, to keep the guns firing at no matter what cost; throwing back in their turn a fearful barrage, pouring frightful punishment upon the heads of the allied soldiers who threw themselves, in waves, over and over for ever, at those awful walls, like the enormous reiteration of a ponderous and terrible symphony, or some ghastly parody of a primitive gigantic ritual or dance.

The ritual went on; the Russian defenders laboured, and behind them, inside the walled city, the rest of their army was preparing, at last, to leave the fortress.

Directly across the harbour from Sebastopol, upon the northern shore, stood her sister fort, the Star. This was to be the escape route. In secrecy and stealth, under Prince Gorchakov's orders, a bridge of boats was lashed together and laid across the water to the haven of the other fort.

Count Tolstoy and another young Russian officer stood at a vantage point on the heights of the Star, and looked across at Sebastopol. As they watched, marching across the bridge of boats to the northern shore, came the remnants of the Russian garrison.

They marched steadily, in filthy rags of uniform, with no soles to their boots. They were young, simple, often illiterate. They came from their homes, the farms, the hamlets, to fight for Holy Russia and the Little Father, as they had been told to do. The tired feet, booted and bootless, trudged across, and behind them, on the outer walls, the brave defenders of the fort stayed to the last, beside their guns.

One by one, the men came to the end of the

bridge of boats. Count Tolstoy, watching, saw that each Russian soldier, as he stepped ashore, made upon his breast the sign of the cross.

Now, in the field hospitals at Balaclava, the casualties came in and there was no more on-duty nor off-duty.

The wounded came in numbers and at speed, in the night, and in the day; there seemed no end to the river of broken bodies that flowed through the place. There was not enough of anything—medicines, drugs, bandages, hands to help; rest for the nurses was an hour snatched here and there, guiltily, when the feet could go no further and the head swam in emptiness.

Tess's back ached and her heart ached, and both did their best to torment her. Those apple-sized Russian bullets had done their work. She tried, with courage, with coolness, to adjust her mind—to accept reality, but she could not become used to the number of amputations. Even the experience of Scutari had not prepared her for it; it seemed that every man who arrived at the field hospitals came with smashed and shattered arms and legs. Hour after hour the surgeons worked on in a desperate race against the raging spread of gangrene; for if the race were lost, then death must surely follow. The operating rooms became chambers of horror in her exhausted eyes. Wounded men lay outside the doors, in the corridors; an ever-continuing stream of smoke-grimed orderlies tramped in, deposited their burdens and returned for more.

The supply of chloroform, always meagre, was finished. Some of the surgeons were not unduly concerned by this; many, indeed, did not bother with the newfangled anaesthesia at all, but rather regarded its use with suspicion, holding to the belief that the shock of the knife was a valuable stimulus to a sinking patient. Roger, however, was not of this opinion; he could not feel that the infliction of pain could be anything but harmful to a human being. Watching him, Tess knew that the sight and sound of agony turned him sick, but he worked on, calm and strong, the brave heart driving on the weary body. She had known him always to be worthy of her respect; the feeling was enriched and deepened as she watched him through those days and, in all the years of her life to come, it would remain with her.

She was standing behind him in one of the operating rooms, when a young soldier, who appeared unconscious, was carried in. The limp body was lifted to the table. The head fell back; the soldier's features were grey, and his hair matted with sweat. One of his arms slipped over the table's edge.

Tess moved forward to lay the arm into place and, as she did so, the closed eyes opened suddenly and stared straight at her. The eyeballs bulged and swivelled about the room; he saw the buckets, the instruments laid ready, the surgical saws.

The soldier's mouth opened wide; the sinews stood out on his neck. Tess fell back, startled, at the hoarse shout that tore itself from his throat.

'No! No! Keep away!'

He flailed his arms, and in a frenzied burst of energy, thrust himself into a sitting position.

'Not my leg—don't take my leg!'

Roger stepped to the head of the table. He looked at the man with hollow eyes.

'I am sorry. It must be done.'

'No—!' The sick man shook his head, in despair and wild defiance. 'Get away, sawbones! Don't you dare touch me!'

Roger was yellow with fatigue. His jaw above the stained brown apron was unshaven and taut across the bone. He brushed the back of a hand across his forehead, and spoke with patient gentleness.

'The leg is smashed. Believe me, this is your only chance. There is gangrene already—'

It was true. The sick smell of putrefaction was thick in the air. Roger went on quietly,

'If there were any other way . . . But there is none. I must take the leg off.'

The soldier burst out into frantic sobs.

'Then I'll die—let me die! Curse you—keep away! I'd sooner die . . .'

Roger regarded him in silence for a moment.

A muscle jerked in his jaw. Suddenly he stepped close, and advanced his face to within a few inches of the other's.

'Listen, will you.' Slowly and distinctly he enunciated each syllable. 'I am going to take that leg off. That's the first thing. Second—I have no chloroform. Do you understand?'

The soldier gulped. His mouth dropped open; his protruding eyeballs were held by that compelling stare.

'You have come so far; now you must go the rest,' Roger went on steadily. 'Of course—you will be a cripple—'

The soldier gasped aloud, and reared up his head in shock. Tess turned a shade whiter; the orderlies stood with impassive faces.

'But—you'll be alive. You will breathe English air . . .' He moved sharply and gripped the slack-jawed man by the shoulders. 'Think, man!' He shook the soldier, gently, but with urgency. 'Think—and answer me the truth! Do you want to die—here—now? In this place?'

In the long pause that followed, the two young men looked into each other's eyes. They were almost of an age. At last, the soldier drew in a long breath; bit his lip; swallowed, and whispered hoarsely,

'Gawd's truth . . . I don't—'

Roger's fingers released their grip, his eyes held the other's. At a jerk of his chin, the orderlies moved forward.

Still looking at Roger's face, the soldier spoke. 'How—how long will it—?'

Between his teeth, the surgeon said briefly, 'It will be quick.'

He gave a signal; the orderlies threw their weight across the body on the table. Tess's palms were sweating. She wiped them on her apron; and moved quietly to her place . . .

Tess moved in a trance of fatigue to the door of the hospital. She stepped outside, and stood against the outer wall, leaning her head back with lids half-closed. Her eyeballs prickled with weariness, the sigh that she uttered came from the very soles of her feet.

Not far from the door a couple of carts were drawn up, and some orderlies were in the fore-court, moving about in an evening hospital ritual. The carts would go on from each hospital to the next; at every stop, a procession of muffled forms would be carried out and placed on the open trays, side by side. They would be borne away, over the sea, to the graves that had been dug for them. There, at Therapia, they would wait, in the stillness of the cemetery, for the service of committal—side by side; resting serenely together—like friends, or brothers.

The wooden carts creaked away. Tess turned her eyes to the night sky and breathed in long and deep. In the heavens the moon was rising slowly, behind some streaming clouds; suddenly these parted, and a brilliant star shone through. Out upon the bay she could see Lord Cardigan's impressive yacht riding at anchor. Two or three other yachts were scattered about on the dark pearly waters. They were black shapes against the sky, showing pinpoints of light from mast-head and porthole. From them, across the water, the sounds of voices sporadically carried to the land.

They were cheerful voices. A noisy burst of shouting and laughter swelled boisterously to the shore. Behind her, Grindle spoke.

'The officers are having a fine old time, it sounds like!'

Another wave of merriment floated to them.

'Half their luck,' Grindle said, with envy. 'I wouldn't mind a drop of what that lot are drink-ing, straight I wouldn't.'

Tess gave a sudden shuddering yawn. Grindle turned on her sharply.

'You're tired out—and you ain't even got your cloak on!' He scolded. 'What are you standing out here for? Come to the kitchen and get some food!'

She smiled at the anxious old face, and said obediently, 'You are right. I'll go in now.'

As she turned to the entrance, there was a movement in the forecourt—a faint jangle of spurred heels, and footsteps on the stones. From the shadows, a tall figure materialised.

Watching as it took shape and came towards

them, Grindle said under his breath,

'Ho! What've we got here, then?'

He looked askance at the newcomer, and scuttled hastily out of sight—but not out of earshot.

Travis Hemrick said, 'Good evening, Lady Eustacia.'

If she made any reply, Grindle, listening with ears pricked, could not distinguish it.

Hemrick said smoothly, 'Will you honour me by accepting this trifle?'

From behind his back, he produced an elegant and expensive basket of sweets and bonbons.

Tess looked in silence at the be-ribboned and tinselled object. Somewhere, in the depths of the building at her back, a man gave a faint groan. At last, she spoke, with biting scorn.

'You are quite contemptible, are you not?'

He bowed; the red mouth was sucked in sharply. When he straightened and spoke, however, his voice was pleasant.

'I beg your pardon, ma'am. I thought only to please you. Is there nothing I may bring that you will accept?'

'Nothing!' She snapped. She moved to leave him, then paused, looking back. 'Nothing . . . At least—'

He was all eagerness.

'Yes? Only name it! It is yours!'

'No! It is useless—you would not, if you could!'

'Won't you tell me? I shall do my utmost, I promise you!'

She swung to face him; her eyes flashed.

'How selfish you are! If you thought of anything except your own pleasure, I should not have to tell you! I want chloroform!'

He was mystified.

'Chloroform? Why do you wish for that?'

'Because there is none in the hospital, nor laudanum either. Not,' added Tess, looking icy daggers at him, 'that one would ever expect a creature such as you to think of that!'

The listener in the darkened hall shot his eyebrows up in admiration.

Sweeping past the disconcerted Captain, Tess departed. Hemrick stood in thought, rubbing his nose, for a minute or two before taking himself off in some disarray.

'One in the eye for you, my lad!' chortled the gleeful eavesdropper.

It was two or three days later that Tess was waylaid by a trooper whom she did not recognise. She looked at the man in faint surprise.

The man proffered a rather bulky bundle.

'Captain Hemrick's compliments, my lady.'

She brushed a weary hand across her eyes.

'I don't want it. Tell Captain Hemrick so.'

'Beg your pardon, ma'am, but the Captain said I was to be sure and give it to you. He said that you would be very pleased to have it.'

Tess stared suspiciously at the cloth-wrapped bundle.

'It's chloroform, my lady—'

'What!'

She reached for the bundle and put aside the cover. A large flagon was revealed. Gingerly she sniffed at the stopper.

'Good God! So it is!'

'There's laudanum coming. The Captain said to tell your ladyship that he would bring it himself when—'

The trooper spoke to empty air.

With both arms around the precious bottle, clutching it tightly to her breast, Tess was already halfway along the hall. With a flick of grey skirt she sped round a corner and vanished.

Roger's eyes popped as she put the flagon into his hands.

'*Hemrick?* Hemrick actually brought this to us?'

'There's laudanum coming as well, so his man said.'

'Well!' With most tender care, Roger took the flagon and set it down as delicately as if it had been fashioned of the finest glass. 'Hemrick! I never would have thought that he . . . . We are in his debt, indeed!'

'Humph!' ejaculated Tess. She cast a darkling look at her beloved, and muttered crossly, 'How stupid men are!'

A gleam of comprehension shot across

Roger's face. He looked at her with amusement in his eye; involuntarily she smiled in response; a spark leapt instantly between them. It warmed them both. Roger lost some of his white and haggard look and, as Tess hurried away, the little smile lingered about her lips; the small spontaneous moment that they had shared stayed with her, comfortably in her heart, for a long time.

CHAPTER
TEN

MRS THIELE lay quite still in her bed, except for one hand that plucked at the covers. Her eyes were open, but they held no comprehension. The firm buxom flesh that had clothed her bones had fallen away, and the rosy skin of her complexion had sagged into greyish lines. The hand on the blanket was yellow and bony.

Murmuring softly, Tess held a spoon to the pale mouth. The thin body that she supported on her shoulder seemed almost light against her own.

The door of the sickroom quietly opened, and Roger entered the room. He approached the bed and bent over the ill woman, taking her hand in his own. The lamplight fell on his head and hands.

'She can barely swallow,' whispered Tess.

He studied the face resting on her shoulder. With his free hand he smoothed back a lock of hair from Mrs Thiele's forehead. It had been pretty hair, glossy and dark, now it hung lank and sweat-soaked. The young man's gesture held an infinity of compassion.

Without speaking, he motioned Tess to lay the sick nurse down. He withdrew beyond the circle of lamplight, and beckoned Tess to join him. They moved to the door and stood together close outside, Tess holding the door ajar, and keeping the sickbed in her line of vision.

Roger said in an undertone, 'She has taken the disease very badly—'

'But she was so strong!'

'I know . . . It happens like that, sometimes.'

Tess swallowed a lump in her throat.

'It seems so unfair . . . But she will rally, won't she? Now that the fever has gone?'

'Certainly she may do so,' he answered, with gentleness. 'We can only hope—and wait.'

Tess turned her eyes and looked sadly into his face.

The longing to lean against him, to rest on his heart and let all her weariness and depression soak away, to break down and cry for a long time with her face on his breast, was a physical pain that stabbed her through. Her mouth quivered. She sensed that he knew her need, and almost imperceptibly he seemed to move towards her; his fingers brushed her own. He said nothing with his lips, but she heard his words in her heart, all the same.

'Tess—my own dear love . . .'

He said gently, 'There are wagons coming in. I must go.'

She held the door a little open, pressing her

face to the aperture, and watched him walk away. Then she breathed in on a sigh, gave herself a hard mental shake, and returned to the sickbed.

Mrs Thiele had closed her eyes, and the restless hand was lax on the covers. Her face twitched a little, and now and then a harsh inhalation lifted her breast. Tess wrung out a cloth in lavender-water and sponged her face, speaking softly the while, but there was no visible response.

She jumped as a sudden imperious voice spoke behind her.

'I want to speak to you!'

She spun about. He was close behind her. The door of the sickroom swung carelessly wide. Her lips parted, she stiffened in incredulous outrage.

'You—how *dare* you! Leave this room instantly!'

Travis Hemrick looked at her in pained surprise.

'What's the matter?' He made no attempt to lower his voice. 'I waited until the sawbones had left!'

Her cheeks began to flame. She said in a furious undertone, 'Your effrontery is past belief!'

'When may I speak to you?'

'Never!'

'Then I'll stay here.' Hemrick picked up the single chair that the room contained and turned it about, scraping it noisily on the floorboards as he did so. He straddled the chair and sat down facing her, legs outstretched.

'Tell me when you finish duty,' he demanded, 'or I shall sit here until you do.'

A mist of rage swam before Tess's eyes. Her immediate impulse was to tear him limb from limb. He watched her, grinning. She bit her lips and bunched her hands. A rasping breath sounded from the bed. She sent a desperate glance at the sick woman, and looked back at Hemrick. He smirked at her.

'When? Tell me!'

Quivering with fury, she spat, 'In two hours. Get *out*!'

He rose, bowed, and went out of the room, pausing in the doorway.

'Really—you are quite magnificent in a rage, you know.'

Tess had already turned back to the sickbed.

When later she emerged from the room, she saw him standing some little distance away in the passage. She attempted to brush by him; he caught her arm.

'Lady Eustacia,' he said, close against her ear. 'Either you grant me a few minutes' private speech, or I shall follow you about the hospital.'

Suddenly Tess was unbearably, unutterably weary. She had not slept, nor had she eaten, for many hours. Her feet seemed no longer to be attached to the rest of her; the cap was heavy on her head—her very braids were weighing her down. She closed her eyes, and rubbed them with her knuckles.

'Very well . . . If only it will rid me of you.'

Hemrick drew her into an empty room off the hall, and carefully closed the door.

'Say what you must and let me be. I am very tired.'

'I could wish that the surroundings were more apt—'

'For heaven's sake! I have told you I am tired!'

'My father's dead.'

With the courtesy that had been bred into her, she answered mechanically,

'I am sorry. Pray accept my condolences.'

'Oh! No need for that,' he said, carelessly. 'Don't believe the old man threw me a civil word since the day I was born. Point is—I'm going back to England—resigning my commission. Son and heir, you know.'

'I wish you a pleasant journey. And now—'

'I sail for England in a few days' time. I am asking you to come with me.'

She made no reply, but turned her back and reached for the door-handle.

'As my wife,' he added hastily, and stepped in front of her.

Tess stared.

'I think you must be mad.'

He spoke suavely, with an ingratiating smile.

'I am asking you to honour me, Lady Eustacia,

by accepting my hand in marriage.'

'Captain Hemrick.' Tess kept her voice level, despite the threatening tremor of a gigantic yawn. 'Kindly stand aside. I am in need of rest.'

'There is a parson in Constantinople who will marry us.' He ignored her words. 'True, you are under age; but since you are here alone, without protection, your father's consent may be dispensed with. On our arrival home, we may go through a formal ceremony, if you wish.'

She looked at him incredulously. In spite of her exhaustion, her temper began to rise.

'Let me pass! I know of no reason why I must stand here and listen to nonsense!'

'Nonsense, is it?' He moved abruptly, and leaned close to her. Something began to smoulder in his hard black eyes. He said softly, 'You are quite a termagant, are you not? And— beautiful, by God!' The next instant he had caught her in a tight embrace.

She tensed her muscles and stood stiff in his arms. His hot breath smelt of brandy. She said, deliberately,

'What a very stupid man you are.'

His mouth twisted; he exhaled a sibilant breath. Nevertheless, he slackened his hold.

'I don't understand you,' he said, on a note of petulance. 'Surely, you can see that we should suit each other admirably? I have no time for the

inane boredom of London society; while you
. . . as for you—'

She tried to release herself, but his hands
tightened on her waist. She stood rigid, disdain-
ing to struggle.

His eyes shifted in the half-light; something
like a leer passed across his face.

'You yourself are—unusual, isn't it so? If
not—you would scarcely be. here . . . *nursing*
naked men.' Squinting sidelong into her eyes,
for a moment he looked like a satyr. 'You
obviously have a taste for . . . the uncommon,
have you not? Or even—shall we say—the
bizarre?' He began to breathe faster. 'Have no
fear, my lady! I am fully able to indulge you in
any—secret appetites that you may have, under
that angel face. I think that you may find it—
interesting . . .'

Tess stared at him. Her face was utterly blank.

He looked her over with narrow eyes; he wore
a puzzled air. After a minute or two, however, he
broke into a snigger.

'Ah—now I see!' He looked at her with dawn-
ing comprehension. 'The handsome surgeon—
of course!' He laughed widely, showing sharp
white teeth. 'So! Cumnor's daughter is titillated
by the vulgar! Well, well!' He patted her arm. 'I
perfectly understand, my dear. A sawbones, a
sturdy groom . . . a lady must have her little
diversions, must she not? I don't begrudge you,
though you will have to forgo such frivolous

pastimes, my love, when we are married—at least until you have provided me with an heir! But I do not think—no, I really do not think you will find yourself too sorely deprived!'

He encountered a look that made him goggle.

For a moment, he was almost afraid. Her eyes flared with a deadly fire; stabbed him with twin shafts of blue lightning. Involuntarily, he stepped back.

She walked, unimpeded, to the door. Each syllable, as she addressed him, fell separately into the air.

'You are totally offensive, sir. Do not approach me again.'

With no further word she left him. He followed after her, for a few paces, along the hall.

'Lady Eustacia . . . Wait—!'

The door of the nurses' dormitory shut crisply behind her.

Grindle, walking from the direction of the kitchens, was carefully carrying a plate of beef and a slice of bread, and grumbling quietly under his breath—For well I know that she won't be bothered to fetch it for herself . . . Faced with the closed door of the dormitory, he came to a halt and proceeded to transfer both plates to one arm, balancing them with some difficulty. Looking up from this operation, he glanced along the hall and saw Hemrick standing a few yards away.

The light was poor, but it was sufficient for Grindle to see the expression on the officer's face. Something ugly, almost menacing, in the way the dashing Captain was regarding that closed door caused Grindle to suffer an uneasy twinge.

Hemrick swung on his heel and stalked away. Grindle gazed after him. He did not know what the Captain could be doing there, outside that door, late at night; nor, in general, would he particularly have cared. But he did not like the look in the Captain's eye, and the longer he thought about it, the less he liked it.

It was the dark of the night when a handful of British soldiers set out to climb the walls of Sebastopol.

On the fortified ramparts that towered above, the Russian guns had stopped at last. The mad cacophony of the allied barrage that thundered death on the heads of those who defended the fort, through days and nights and dawns and twilights, had finally died away. From high up in the sky there came no reply, no sound, nothing at all, only darkness, and a cold silence that entered the heart and chilled it—absolute and profound, in contrast to what had gone before.

Down below in the allied lines, the final assault, the last great victory which would be blazoned across the pages of history and rest in crimson and gold on the royal brow of Louis Napoleon, was decided upon. It was to be at dawn. The die was cast.

Around them, the wind had hushed somewhat, and about the great fortress, nothing moved nor stirred. The quietness seemed heavy, ominous; in the allied camp, the question grew— were the guns broken at last, or were the Russians waiting? Lord Raglan's men had met death in that other dawn . . . was that to be repeated? The question grew more imperative as the hours passed; it had to be answered.

Following their young officer, the band of volunteers crawled up and over the tops of the trenches and out into the bleak scarred no-man's-land which had to be crossed. There were ditches twenty feet deep, with yellow stinking mud in the bottom; the men slipped and floundered through, with clogged eyes and noses, cursing under their breath . . . There were exposed stretches of torn-up, unsteady ground, strewn with rubble to trip and gash, and of a certainty booby-trapped and mined.

The volunteers went on, sliding, inching on their bellies, muddied and slimed from head to foot, while above, the outer walls waited—the walls that would, if the Russian gunners were foxing, lead them upwards to certain death.

As they began to climb, a cold and watery moon came out between racing streams of cloud. The wind began beating on the walls, assaulting the men, swirling up from the dark depths below them; it made a hoarse deep whistle and, as they went higher, it caught at them, howling, and froze their hands. Their feet slipped on the wet stone, and a bayonet struck icy rock with a shivering jangle.

Above their upturned faces, the fort seemed not to decrease in height but rather to sweep to the heavens, wider, higher; but still they went on, scrabbling their way up the ascent of brick and stone, conscious of the massive size and thickness of it. Even their breathing seemed muted and subdued, as if the gigantic bulk had by contrast reduced their bodies and shrunken them.

On they went, and higher, and came at last to the uppermost embrasures—and still they heard nothing.

They paused, then, listening to the silence.

The leading man stood up, was outlined against the sky, and dropped down softly into the fort. One by one, catlike, the others followed. With eyes turning, they crouched together, looking about them.

There was nothing there.

Only the wind blew; only the rats moved.

And so Sebastopol was taken.

When the main body of the allies entered the city at daylight, they found that they had captured a ruin. The place was blackened and empty. Every ship of war in the harbour, every battery and magazine, had been destroyed. Only the dead were left. There was a burial place within the city walls, that the Russians them-

selves had named the Cemetery of the Hundred
Thousand.

That was the victory of Sebastopol.

In the summer that was to follow, something
strange was seen to happen in the Crimea.

The crocuses, the hyacinths, the vines
sprouted and grew, and that was as usual, but, as
well as that, long black squadrons of kites and
ravens and vultures, of a size and number that
had never been seen in living memory, came
hovering, swishing and flapping over the battle-
fields. Some of the vultures, it was said, had
flown all the way from Africa.

Emperor Napoleon III (valiant to the last)
urged his General to chase the Russians into
their own land. But General Pélissier was not
likely to fall into that trap. It was already
September, and soon the deadly winter would
come down—blasting across those limitless
plains, blotting out life. Pélissier was not to be
tempted into that freezing inferno.

Negotiations began . . . for peace.

The arguments and the wrangling went on,
and on, and stretched into weeks, and months.

The British army, then, was destined to wait in
the Crimea, spending another winter upon the
shores of the Bay.

This time, however, they lived through the
bitter months in comfortable well-warmed huts,
with plentiful food and heavy woollen clothing.
The near-by hospitals remained, fully equipped

and functioning, for any needs that might arise—according to the word of Miss Florence Nightingale.

The Treaty was signed at last, in Paris, in the March of 1856. Among other things it laid down that the great naval dockyard of Sebastopol was to be abolished and to remain so—for ever.

CHAPTER
ELEVEN

THE NURSE Mary whispered, 'Is there any change?'

'No. She has not awakened.'

'She rests quietly . . .'

'Yes.' Tess set down the bedside lamp. 'There does not seem to be any pain. For that, at least, we may be thankful. I'll be back at midnight.'

In the nurses' dormitory, Tess opened the window a little and rested her elbows on the sill. The night was growing colder and a sea-wind curled rather eerily about the huts. It blew past the window, catching at her hair.

Suddenly, on the back of the wind, a note of music came to her. She listened, looking across the quadrangle to the low outline of a newly-constructed barrack hut which housed some of the enlisted men. Turning her head to catch the sound, she heard through the dark a few bars of melody. She smiled. The statesmen of Europe were disagreeing around the conference tables and, in the meantime, the army must wait here. But the men, snug in their cosy quarters, did not seem to mind so very much, she thought.

Light glowed from the windows of the hut, directly opposite to where she stood; laughter and cheerful voices drifted through the night. Louder and clearer, she heard again the strains of music . . . someone was playing upon a violin.

The song was a simple country tune she had known from her childhood. Leaning forward, arms crossed on the sill, she began—very softly —to hum the refrain. The dark compound faded, and for a minute or two she saw another time and place. She was ten years old and her hand was firmly enclosed in Nurse's; around her on a summer Yorkshire afternoon a country fair was in full swing. There were bright-faced girls dancing and laughing, with ribbons bobbing in their hair, and the fiddlers played for dear life, flashing their teeth and flourishing their bows— and all about her, seeming magic to her child's eyes, were colours, and shouting, and jovial faces—the air was full of joyousness. She dimpled at the memory, and sighed a little, listening at the window.

She looked out again across the deserted square . . . It was, after all, not so very far! A deep chorus of voices rose up, with the brave note of the violin.

For a moment longer, she hesitated, then tossed her cap upon the bed, and turning, caught up her cloak. With her eyes fixed upon the lighted window, well wrapped in the grey cloak, she walked briskly across the compound.

Her pace slowed, however, as she neared the hut. Approaching the closed door, she stood irresolute. The darkness and silence outside was in sharp contrast with the music and cheerful noises that swelled within.

As she lingered, hesitating in front of the door, a footstep sounded behind her. With a faint gasp, she turned; the newcomer came up beside her. She saw that it was Roger.

In a little flutter, with a guilty blush, she said breathlessly,

'Oh, dear! I ought not to be here . . . It was the music—'

'I heard it too.' There was a little pause. Roger went on quietly,

'To hear music in this place—it took me home, to the dancing, the fair. That tune—I know it well.'

'So do I,' she said eagerly. 'Oh! How well I remember . . .' She looked at the closed door. 'Could we—could we go in, do you think?'

Roger's eyes began to twinkle. His face split into a boyish grin.

'Why not?' He pushed the door open.

Within the hut there was life and good cheer. A well-stoked brazier burned in the middle of the floor. Around this, in the comfortable warmth, a group of soldiers were sitting.

The brazier glowed bright red, and lit up the circle of faces.

Tess looked about her, and her eyes suddenly

danced as she saw that the player was Grindle. The little man was perched upon a stool, with the pretty polished instrument tucked under his chin, and his gnarled fingers were moving over the strings with a skill that surprised her. Briefly she wondered how Grindle could have come by so unlikely a possession and decided that it would be more tactful, perhaps, not to ask.

The tune trilled in the air, and the men sang and snapped their fingers with the rhythm. Tess and Roger took a step further into the room. For a few moments they stood unnoticed by the singers. Then Grindle looked up, and saw the watching figures outside the brazier's circle of light.

His face creased in welcome, and heads turned. Instantly there was a concerted movement and stir.

'Come in, come in!'

'Come and join us—'

'Over here!'

'Make room for the doctor and the nurse—'

'Here—come and sit here!'

Room was made for them in the circle; they were ushered to a place of honour. With as much ceremony as if they had been her courtiers and she a queen, two burly troopers spread a blanket for Tess to sit on. She seated herself, a little shyly, murmuring her thanks. Roger took his place beside her. Her skirt brushed his knee, their shoulders were almost touching in the dimness. The men settled back into their places.

A lantern had been hung up on a post. This, together with the burning coals in the brazier, illuminated the faces around them. One or two of them were known to Tess by sight. She distinguished the features of a young corporal who earlier in the day had brought her a letter from his wife, asking her if she would read it aloud, explaining that he had always found it hard to con the words. The soldier smiled at her; she returned the smile.

Grindle shouted, 'Now then, boys!'

Heartily, in unison, the voices rose. The hut filled with sound.

Tess was suddenly gripped by the remembrance of so many who were gone, and of all that had been wasted in their going. Her eyes stung and she saw the faces of the singers through a mist. But at the same time, as she listened and watched, another feeling stole over her. It was as if she saw something else, without knowing what it was—perhaps it was courage, or love. She could not name it; but she knew that it was a truth that would stay with her, and be remembered, helping her always to comprehend the human heart and understand the pain and the bravery of it. Without knowing it, her hand reached out to Roger's. Their palms touched, and clung; his fingers closed on hers and interlaced with them. Warmth flowed between them through the clasped hands.

The music ended with a rousing chord on the fiddle. Somebody called out,

'Pearce—Will Pearce! Where are you? Stand up, boy!'

At the back of the room, a youthful soldier was urged to his feet, and propelled forward by friendly hands. The soldier's features still bore traces of the chubbiness of boyhood and his manly beard was the merest goose-down. He hung his head, rather awkward and sheepish, while jovial exhortations rose about him.

'Sing up, boy!' 'Don't be bashful—give us a song!' 'Give us "Barbara Allen" . . . Come on, Will!'

Thus adjured, and seeing there was no escape, he lifted up his head and began to sing, alone and unaccompanied.

'"Twas in about the Mart'nmas time, when the red leaves were fallin'"', sang the child-soldier.

At the first note, all conversation ceased. Tess's head sank upon Roger's shoulder. The voice was a true tenor, innocent and untrained; the sexless clarity of childhood was still in it. The boy stood leaning against the post where the lantern hung. The light just missed him; his face was in shadow. Lovely and haunting the old ballad rose—to the rafters and beyond, through the night and into the sky. There was no applause when the song was finished, nobody moved or spoke as the young voice died away into quietness.

Blushing, the lad retired to the back of the room and resumed his seat amid comradely pats on the shoulders and approving smiles. He declined, for the present, to give an encore, but promised, with becoming modesty, to sing again 'in a while—if you still want it'.

Grindle took up the fiddle and struck up a leaping jigging tune. Immediately the room came to life. Heavy feet began to stamp the floorboards, hands beating time, it was a rousing country dance.

The sprightly notes caught at Tess's toes and set them involuntarily tapping.

The music rose, exciting, exuberant; the noise swelled; the hut rocked to a crescendo of rhythmic feet, hands and voices.

Roger's hand quivered in her own. Suddenly, he leaped to his feet, and swept her a bow. His teeth gleamed, and his eyes, laughing, challenging, invited her to the dance.

Tess gasped,

'Oh—! I—I should not—'

She looked around her, saw nodding heads and smiles; a shout of encouragement ran round the group; the music rose and reverberated. Roger offered his arm.

Tess caught her breath and laughed aloud. She tossed her cloak aside, sprang into the circle and bobbed a curtsy to her love.

In an instant they were dancing, surrounded by a ring of clapping, tapping admirers. Up and down, round and round, went Tess and Roger, skipping, turning, stamping. Their flying figures were silhouetted against the ruddy light of the glowing embers. Their eyes were flashing, laughing, each at the other; Roger's brown hair tossed back from his forehead—the years fell away from his face, leaving it boyish, young, alive . . . Together, they glowed and sparkled; the music spoke of love, and life and joyousness; in the circle of light, they were alone, outside time, and loss, and sadness . . .

The music tantalised, beckoned and thrilled; and when the dance ended at last, they stood in the circle in a wave of friendly applause. With a final pirouette and flourish, Tess swept her partner a formal curtsy; flushed and dimpling, her eyes shining into his, she rose—and saw, beyond his shoulder, the face of an orderly who had pushed open the door at the end of the room and was making his way towards them.

Roger turned, and saw the man approaching.

A few words were exchanged in an undertone. Roger turned back to Tess. The laughter had gone from his eyes; his face was grave.

'I am needed urgently, Tess, in the operating room—'

She said instantly, 'I will come with you.'

He looked at her for a thoughtful moment, at the delicate colour in her cheeks, the soft hurried breath, the sweet dishevelment of the severely braided hair.

'No. You stay. Enjoy the music! Grindle will bring you back across the compound.' He added, with compunction, 'God knows, you have had little enough to lift your spirits these past weeks.'

'I really should not—'

'Of course you should . . .' He pressed her hand and nodded to the orderly. The door closed behind them; he was gone.

Tess turned back rather slowly into the circle. The violin was playing quietly, nostalgically, under Grindle's caressing hands. She sat down again beside the place where Roger had been, and clasped her hands around her knees. Friendly faces nodded and smiled and she smiled in return. Presently the boy came from the shadows behind her and sang again. The melody caught at her heart.

Suddenly, she knew that it was no use. He had gone from her side, and without his presence, despite the warm red brazier and the happy voices and the songs, the room was empty, dark and cold. She could not stay . . . there was no happiness there, without him.

The faces around her were absorbed, lost in the melody; Grindle was swaying in time to it, his eyes far off, his hand straying over the strings. Tess rose like a shadow and moved to him, leaning above his shoulder.

She whispered, 'I must leave now.'

Grindle smiled, vaguely, and continued to play. She said, softly, to those in her immediate vicinity, 'Thank you so much. Goodnight.' The music followed her as she glided to the door, opened it noiselessly and slipped away into the night.

Ahead of her, across the square, the hospital windows dimly shone.

As she set out towards them, behind her in the hut the music went on. Some voices picked up the chorus; others joined in.

It was very dark in the square, but the light in front beckoned. Tess turned up her collar and began to walk smartly, eyes on the welcoming glow ahead. The air had become colder, and out on the bay there were white curls of foam on the choppy waves. Tess quickened her steps.

She was almost there; a mere fifty yards separated her from the hospital door.

For a brief second only, she glimpsed the two vague shapes that materialised from the darkness; they came up, one on each side of her. She was fleetingly aware of the sickly sweetness of chloroform as a cloth was pressed hard over her mouth and nose. She knew nothing more.

In the barrack-hut, the men sang on. Their voices mingled with the rising voice of the wind as it keened around the huts, and swept across the quadrangle . . . masking all sound of movement, and carrying it away.

Some of the men were dozing, wrapped in their greatcoats. The brazier had burned low. Grindle ran a loving hand along the bridge of the fiddle, and laid it tenderly in its case.

A sleepy voice asked, with mild curiosity, 'Where'd you get it, Grindle?'

The orderly closed one eye in an exaggerated wink.

'I wangled it, me son,' he grinned. Someone guffawed. Grindle added complacently, 'And when you're an old soldier like me, lad, maybe you'll know how to wangle too.'

He picked up the fiddle-case, tucking it securely under his arm, and quitted the hut. He cocked a knowing eye at the heavens and thought that it looked like sleet before morning.

Hunching himself into his coat, he walked with lowered head and rolled an eye askance towards the Bay. Lord Cardigan's yacht was all in darkness, except for her riding lights; his lordship must be tucked up in bed. There were other ships out there; he picked out the *Dancer*, well away and apart from the rest. With sails reefed and bow-anchor taut, she was riding free, head on to the wind. He could hear the swell slapping the pontoons and the grating of boats against the landing-stage. A storm could be blowing up, he wouldn't be surprised; well, it did not matter to him—he was snug enough here. So were they all, come to that.

The wind was blowing off the sea. As he

entered the hospital a gust caught him and almost lifted him through the door. Arrived in his own quarters, he hid the precious fiddle carefully in the bottom of a canvas bag. A room of his own was another of his successful 'wangles'. It was very small, but a brazier like those in the army huts burned cosily in the corner, and from somewhere or other he had procured an enormous shabby, but eminently comfortable, wingchair.

Grindle removed his tunic, and gave a cavernous yawn. Halfway to the armchair, however, he paused and went to the door. He padded along the hall to Mrs Thiele's room and tapped gently on the panels. To the face that appeared in the aperture, he whispered,

'Just thought I'd ask how the lady is, before I turn in.'

'There is no change,' was the low reply. 'But Grindle—wait a moment. Have you seen Mrs Mainwaring anywhere?'

'She'd be in the dormitory, wouldn't she? Why?'

'Oh—it's nothing. Only—she was to return at midnight, and she has not come. It is long past the hour.'

Grindle was startled.

'You mean—she hasn't come to relieve you?'

'No—and it is not like her. She is usually so prompt.'

Grindle screwed up his face in bewilderment.

'You're right—it ain't like her at all. Maybe she laid down for a rest, and dozed off, like. I'll cut along and see. Can you carry on here for a bit?'

'Oh—certainly. When all's said and done, there's little that I can do here,' replied Mary, sadly. 'If you find Tess sleeping, don't disturb her, Grindle. I am not at all tired. I only wondered why she had not come, that is all.'

'I'll find out.'

He limped towards the nurses' room, and came to the closed door. He pressed an ear to the panel and, after listening for a moment or two, cautiously pushed the door open. Peering round, he saw that some of the beds were occupied, and sounds of regular breathing bore testimony to deep slumber. In the dim rays of the nightlamp, he stole past them and reached the end of the room.

Grindle pulled up short and stood, with dropped mouth, staring at Tess's empty bed.

Roger Verrall's shoulder was shaken by an ungentle hand.

'Sir! Sir! Wake up!'

Roger opened his eyes. Grindle's face was hovering above him.

'Wake up—for God's sake! She's gone!'

'Who—?'

'Nurse Mainwaring, sir—gone!'

'*What!*'

The old man groaned aloud.

'I blame meself! Holy Christ, what a fool! I should've walked back with her—'

Roger had leaped to the floor and was struggling into his boots.

'It's all my fault . . .' Grindle wailed. 'Sir—we have got to hurry! I've brought me pistols. There's a swell running, but we can take the supply boat—the two of us can handle it! Lord, Lord—why didn't I bring her back meself! But I never thought he'd—'

Snatching up his tunic, Roger snapped, 'Don't stand there babbling! Search the wards—the kitchens—'

Grindle cried out in despair.

'Sir, I *have*—she ain't there! I'm trying to tell you! He's anchored well out, and the minute the wind swings round, he'll be away! We've got to—'

'What are you talking about! Make sense!'

'I been watching him—I suspicioned all along that he was one who'd move all hell to get his own way; but as Gawd's me judge, I never thought he'd have the nerve to—' He stopped, and threw up his hands, retreating hastily as Roger took a menacing stride in his direction. 'In short,' he gabbled, 'don't ask me how I know— it's a feeling I've had in me guts! But I know I'm right—Sir! It's Hemrick who has done this!'

Tess was whirling and spinning headlong through a vortex. Thin whistling sounds flew past her, interspersed with dizzying bright-coloured circles and patches of blackness. Somewhere ahead of her there was a continuing glow; her eyes were shut, but she could see it through the closed lids . . . she was being rushed towards it, without volition. She tried to hold back, to steady herself, but her arms were heavy and would not move.

She opened her mouth, gasping and fighting for breath, and came up into the light.

Somewhere over her head a lamp was suspended. It was swinging a little, and it hurt her eyes. She tried to lift a wooden hand against the dazzle. She seemed, however, to be resting on something yielding and comfortable; this was pleasant, and rather soothing. She felt reassured. She did not, as yet, know where she was, but the problem did not seem urgent; she decided for the moment not to bother about it.

Without interest, she became aware that a voice was speaking her name. Its owner appeared to expect an answer, and this was tedious. She paid no attention. A hand was shaking her shoulder; apparently this annoying person—whoever he might be—expected her to awaken. Well, she would not; it was too much trouble. She mumbled a few disjointed words to that effect, and began to slide away into opaque and whirling mists of delicious sleep.

A hard palm struck her across the face—once, twice. Her head jarred back and forth under the force of the blows. The shock of it drove an involuntary cry from her throat.

From close above her, the voice said, in silky tones,

'You really must wake up, my dear. I have been patient for quite long enough.'

Her eyes flew open to their fullest; they focused, uncertainly, on the face that hung over her. She uttered a faint sound and tried to struggle into a sitting position. Her muscles were weak, her limbs heavy; she fell back, helpless.

'I did not think that you would take so long to come to your senses,' complained Captain Hemrick. 'The fools must have been over-zealous. Still, it does not matter, you will soon be yourself again.' He turned to a nearby table set with glasses and silver. 'You need a restorative, I dare say. Brandy, perhaps?'

With one hand to the back of her head, he pushed the goblet against her mouth, half-choking her, forcing her to swallow. The neat spirit burned her throat. Her blue eyes moved desperately from side to side. She struggled with the fumes, gasping, and at last forced a word to her lips; it came out in a croak.

'Where—?'

'On the *Dancer*, of course,' he answered, smiling.

Tess was lying at full length on a velvet chaise-longue, her head propped up on the padded end-cushion. The saloon in which she lay seemed, as her eyes swivelled round it, to resemble a kaleidoscope of red and gold and ornate gilded carving. The gleaming mirrors on every wall reflected dancing points of light. The whole effect was that of a seraglio. The carpet was deep crimson, silken and thick; chased and gilded lamps, embedded with coloured stones, swung from the ceiling on golden chains. Satin hangings of rich and startling design hung upon the walls, and in the air was a strange, exotic, smell which she did not recognise as incense. It caught at her nostrils; she had a sudden stifled desire for air.

Hemrick replaced the goblet on the gilt-encrusted table, and seated himself at the foot of the chaise-longue.

'You seem puzzled,' he said, solicitously. 'Really, there is no need; I am returning to England, as I told you; and I have not the least intention of going without you . . . Spoils of war, my dear!' He chuckled. 'Nobody knows that you are here; by morning, we shall be well away.' The smiled deepened on his lips, in the soft light of the Byzantine lamps, his eyes looked like polished black buttons. 'I am sure you will enjoy the voyage, my love,' he said, softly. 'We shall be quite snug here together, you and I.'

With eyes strained to their widest, Tess stared at him.

Nobody knew that she was there. As she assimilated the full meaning of his words, a naked icy finger of fear touched her heart. Nobody knew . . . and it was wildly unlikely that she would be missed before morning. True, she would fail to appear in Mrs Thiele's room at midnight; but she realised, with a sinking heart, that good-natured Mary would simply assume that Tess had fallen asleep—it would never occur to her to draw attention to Tess's deficiency, or to complain . . . it would be dawn before it was realised that something was amiss.

With a sort of horror she thought of the hospital, now wrapped in slumber; the dark night outside, the black iridescent waters that separated her from the shore. Her eyes stared into his; she shook her head with a convulsive movement, and worked her mouth, trying to speak; but no words came.

Hemrick watched her with cruel amusement, enjoying the slow realisation of her predicament, as it dawned fully in her face. Suddenly he broke into laughter, and reached out for her. His hands encircled her wrists—he jerked her upright on the couch.

'I have had you watched for days,' he informed her, smiling. 'How obliging of you, my dear, to walk in the compound alone! And now . . . You are here! When we reach Constantinople, we shall be married.'

Tess pulled back as far as she was able from the bruising grip on her forearms. His physical nearness set every fibre of her body shivering with revulsion. His small full-lipped mouth was wet and red, his eyes held an opaque sheen. Painfully, through her burning throat, she gasped out, 'No! No—I won't—'

'Oh yes, you will,' he assured her. He laughed softly. 'By the time we reach Constantinople, you will be ready—no, anxious—to exchange vows, my lady.'

Somewhere inside her she found a resurgence of strength and began to struggle, angrily, in his grasp. Still laughing, he suddenly twisted her arms behind her back, forcing the wrists up to her shoulderblades.

Involuntarily, her neck arched and her head fell back. He clamped her two hands in one of his own; his other hand touched her hair.

'You see, I have respect for your claws, my love! Now—'

She felt his fingers busy among her braids. Held helpless, shuddering at his touch, she felt the heavy ropes of shining gold fall loose and tumble, one by one, over her shoulders and breast. He caressed the gleaming masses; her flesh crept as his fingers brushed her neck.

'That's much better,' he said, and abruptly released her. 'Really—you are a goddess, my dear Lady Eustacia! We are going to deal *very* well together—believe me!'

He got up, and trod across the carpet to the doorway connecting with an adjoining cabin. The aperture was hung with a shimmering curtain; he brushed it aside and disappeared within.

In a few seconds he emerged, carrying across his arm a satin robe.

'I have only this for you to wear.' His handsome visage wore a bland expression; his smile, however, was feline. 'But you will not need anything more for the present, will you?' He threw the robe across the foot of the couch and stroked the shining folds; they were of peacock blue, and embroidered in silver. He looked at her sidelong. 'Such loveliness should be more fittingly clothed, my dear. Shall we remove those ugly garments you are wearing? You will throw them in the sea. Yes, you yourself . . . one by one. You will enjoy that, won't you?'

Tess's cheeks flamed. She reared up her head, and hissed like a spitting cat.

'You are loathsome! Disgusting! Don't dare come near me!'

He purred, 'Oh, but I shall . . .'

He thrust her back against the head-rest; his weight pinned her against it. His fingers strayed to the collar of her dress.

Frantically she twisted her head away from his lips. Her legs were still weak, but she made a valiant effort to kick out at him.

'Why, that is much better!' he mocked. 'I prefer you to be spirited, my love; I really do not want you to show submissiveness . . .' He sat back, letting his gaze travel the length of her body, insolently and lingeringly. He noted with approval the angry colour mantling her cheeks, and the flame in her blue eyes.

He said, 'On second thoughts . . . We need not rush our pleasure, after all—need we? I can see that you are recovering. In a little while—when you are feeling strong again—we shall enjoy much better sport . . . I do like, you know, to savour things . . .' He got up, still smiling, and turned to the table. 'In the meantime—some wine, perhaps? Or may I offer you some of this caviar? It is delicious.'

He was in the act of raising a morsel to his mouth when Roger Verrall plummeted down the companion-ladder into the saloon.

At the same moment, on the deck above, the sounds of a fracas broke out; there was some scuffling, and a commotion of sorts, at the head of the ladder. Then there was silence.

Hemrick stood open-mouthed and dumb-founded; the mouthful of caviar halfway to his lips.

Roger's booted heels thudded into the carpet. Legs planted wide, head outthrust, his eyes under black-barred brows swept the cabin. The irises were white, almost silver, in the dancing glimmering lamplight.

His searing glance took in the scene. The points of light in those diamond-hard eyes flared into a white flame. For a second Hemrick still stood, nonplussed; in that second Roger moved. The table which barred his path was lifted, con-tents and all, and smashed into the Captain's face. There was a crash, and a splintering of glass. Hemrick's upflung arm saved him a little, but the table-edge took him full in the chest. He staggered back against the wall of the cabin, his forehead cut by a flying glass sliver.

Tess uttered a faint, incredulous, strangled cry, and stretched out two trembling hands. They were taken in a strong, warm clasp. Roger dropped on one knee beside the couch, and smiled into her eyes.

'My darling—you are quite safe now. Stay there just a little moment. Then I'll take you ashore.'

Her eyes moved suddenly to a point beyond his shoulder; she uttered a warning gasp. Roger turned his head and ducked in the nick of time. Hemrick had snatched a sabre from the wall; the blade whistled evilly past the intruder's head.

Roger sprang from the floor and caught the upraised arm. The two men stood, chest to chest. Roger's hand contracted on the other's wrist, forcing the arm with the deadly blade up and back. Hemrick strained and cursed; he could not break the ferocious vice of those surgeon's fingers, nor crack the sinews of that iron wrist. There was a heaving and a gasping, a locked duel of faces glaring one at the other . . . Then the Captain's hand slackened. The weapon slid from his numbed fingers and hit the floor with a soft thump.

Roger dived for it and snatched at the hilt; his

fist closed about it. The next instant, Hemrick found himself at bay with the sabre hard against his throat.

With slitted eyes on his adversary's face, Roger smiled.

His lips were carved back against his teeth, like those of a grinning skull. Softly, through those grinning teeth, Roger said,

'On deck, Captain.'

Step by step, Hemrick retreated; stumbled against the foot of the ladder and climbed it backwards, feeling his way with his feet—forced upwards to the deck by the naked edge of steel beneath his chin.

At the top of the companion-ladder, Grindle was standing. His pistols were trained on a group of deckhands, dimly seen in the shadows aft, behind the stays. As the Captain and Roger hove into view, one or two of the leading hands took a pace forward. Grindle barked,

'Keep back! This ain't nothing to do with you lot! This here is private business between officers!'

His tone, and the rock-steady hands that aimed the pistols at their heads, formed a convincing argument. The men decided not to argue the point, but shrugged their shoulders and retreated, mumbling something to their fellows. The whole group then retired to the sanctuary of the after-deck, where they took up discreet vantage points and settled themselves to follow the

subsequent proceedings with a good deal of interest; and (it must be confessed) an honest
measure of simple enjoyment.

Keeping his eyes on the Captain, Roger stepped to the deckrail and swung the sabre round his
head. It flew through the air, up and out, cart-
wheeling and sending a fleeting dull glimmer
from the curved blade. Then it vanished, with a
distant splash, into the waters of Balaclava Bay.

'Now, you bastard,' said Roger to Captain
Hemrick.

Although Grindle's view of the ensuing con-
test was slightly hampered by the necessity of
keeping his pistols on the watchers in the stern,
he contrived not to miss a moment of it.

The deck was illuminated by the masthead
lanterns, and the light was reasonably adequate.
Sizing up the adversaries with a knowledgeable
eye, Grindle considered that they were pretty
fairly matched. Captain Hemrick was heavier,
and had the advantage of reach, but Mr Verrall
was fast on his feet and mighty powerful in the
legs and shoulders, thought Grindle with expert
appraisal, weighing up the young surgeon's phy-
sique. The Captain rattled in gamely, and landed
a couple of nice flush hits—including a counter-
cross that evoked the orderly's ungrudging respect; Mr Verrall went staggering back into the
shrouds, but bounced back again in a trice and
very soon proceeded to let the Captain have
something to think about.

Back and forward the fight raged in the narrow space. They were pretty even, all told; it boiled down, in the end, to which of them would tire first . . . and it was becoming plain that Captain Hemrick was running out of puff. He began to slow down; Grindle could hear him starting to heave like a blown horse. Gradually, step by step, Mr Verrall drove him backwards until at last he could retreat no farther and came up hard against the wheelhouse.

It was then that Mr Verrall moved in. Lovely to watch, thought Grindle with real appreciation, the way he went about taking the Captain apart. There was the noise of his fists thudding into the Captain's midriff, like a round of gunfire, almost; the Captain doubling up; the uppercut that hit the Captain's unguarded jaw with an audible crack. Mr Verrall grabbed the tottering Captain; jerked him upright; the process was repeated.

'Sir,' said the orderly, tentatively, at last. 'Do you think you oughter—so to speak—roll him up proper?'

Roger straddled the gasping figure crouched up against the wheelhouse. The surgeon was breathing fast, and his face was disfigured by a great livid bruise over the cheekbone. Blood trickled from the corner of his mouth. He looked down at the helpless Captain.

'Perhaps not,' he said at last, with some unwillingness. 'However—' He hoisted the unresisting officer to one shoulder and hauled him across to the deckrail, balancing him there for a moment. 'This may cool him down,' said Roger, and gave his victim a hearty shove.

There was a brief struggle, a frantic flailing of arms and legs and a loud splash. Captain Hemrick had fallen overboard.

A commotion of sorts broke out on the afterdeck. There were exclamations, some stifled laughter, the sounds of running feet. Someone came running with a boathook, and there were sundry threshings, splashings and cursings as Hemrick's minions fished for him in Balaclava Bay.

'Y'know what, sir?' remarked Grindle, elbow on rail, watching this activity with interest. 'I don't believe as how the Captain can swim.'

There was no reply. Roger had vanished down the companionway.

Tess was standing in the saloon with her eyes glued to the point where the steps disappeared upwards. Her head had stopped its silly wobbling, and she thought, as she measured the height of the stairs, that she probably could negotiate them and clamber up to the deck. But—he had asked her to stay where she was. She stood without moving, therefore, white-faced, clasping and unclasping her hands, and straining for sounds from above, with her gaze painfully riveted on the ladder.

He came down, and she cried out at the marks

of combat on his face. She was lifted, borne willy-nilly up the stairs and carried across the deck before she could draw breath. Grindle was already in the boat below and, as she was handed down into it, the dripping form of Captain Hemrick—ignominiously suspended by the seat of his breeches—was dragged up past the freeboard and deposited, weakly swearing and spitting saltwater, on the boat deck.

His erstwhile visitors, however, felt no obligation to stay and assist the Captain in his distress. They shoved off with a will, and bent to the oars.

The Bay had grown rough, and both men were needed to handle the supply boat and keep a steady course. Tess sat on the floor, curled up in the sternsheets, her eyes barely level with the gunwales. Spume and spray hissed about her and blew into her face. The unwieldy flat-bottomed boat lurched and juddered. Her soaked hair dripped on her forehead and neck. She was chilled through, and cramped, and decidedly queasy . . . and never in her life had she been so gloriously, so totally, happy.

Her heart and her head sang with joy; she could have burst with it. She watched Roger's face above her, his head thrown back, the column of his throat where the damp shirt fell away, the surge of strength in shoulder and thigh as he leaned to the oars. Grindle shouted,

'Wind's turning, sir!'

Roger's eyes flashed through the wet brown

elf-locks whipped across his brow. Tess huddled her arms around her knees and did not move her gaze from his face.

The racing current took the boat; it bounded forward through the water. The wind was against them, but the sea was with them.

They bumped at last into the shallows. Grindle hauled on the mooring-rope.

Roger carried her to the shore, wading thigh-deep, lifting her high above the water. Very carefully, very tenderly, he placed her feet on dry land.

Something in her wilting mien alerted Grindle's sharp eye. He touched her shoulders, peering into her averted face. He spoke with sudden urgency.

'Sir—!'

Roger turned his beloved's countenance upwards. There was almost no light, but despite the gloom, he sensed rather than saw the sickly green hue that had overspread her cheeks.

The accumulated effects of drugging, neat brandy, emotional turmoil and the rocking motion of the boat suddenly and imperatively rushed together and would not be denied.

The Lady Eustacia made a helpless gesture, sent each of her companions a tight-lipped little smile and succumbed to the inevitable.

'Marrying a physician has singular advantages,' Tess remarked dreamily. 'For if one is *obliged* to be sick, he knows how to hold one's head, and is not in the least disconcerted.'

Roger chuckled, and hugged her closer to his chest.

They were in Grindle's room. The old man had stocked up the brazier and closed the door firmly upon them. He then stumped along to Mrs Thiele's room, and whispered to the nurse seated beside the bed that Mrs Mainwaring was a little bit unwell; nothing to worry about—should he go and get somebody else? There was no need, Mary assured him; she herself could manage quite well until dawn; someone would come then.

Grindle made his way to the kitchen, to doss down in the warm near one of the fires. En route, he paused by a window and squinted out over the Bay. Rain had begun and was thickening the air; he had to strain his eyes; but faintly, at last, he made out two pinpoints of light, red and green, far out on the moving horizon, as a yacht stood out to sea. He went on his way with a grin of satisfaction. In the kitchen, he settled himself cosily near the hearth, turned up his collar and prepared to doze until morning. His eyes were closed, and his face wore an expression close to beatific.

The lovers were snuggled together in Grindle's vast old wingchair. 'I don't know how he gets these things,' Tess murmured. 'He wangles them,' Roger grinned. The brazier sent forth a bright and heartwarming glow, the wind sang about the building and rattled the frames, the rain hissed over the roofs . . . and Tess, lying on Roger's lap, burrowed closer and pressed her cheek against his heart.

He said, 'It is what I dreamed of—through all the aching hours . . .'

'We shall never be parted again.'

'My life is yours. While I live, no one shall harm you—Tess! My only love—'

They lay in each other's arms in the depths of the old chair, while the sleet came down and joined the land and sea together.

She looked up, questioning, as he stirred. The darkening bruise on his cheek gave him a rakish look, like a young pirate. He said soberly,

'I am afraid that your family will turn away from you.'

She answered, after a moment's thought,

'They won't do that. I am—in fact—not what they expected in a daughter, nor hoped for . . . But they have accepted, I believe, that I—must walk a different road.' Roger nodded.

'When we return home,' Tess went on slowly, 'we shall try to tell them—explain to them— what we have done here . . . what we have seen. They will be shocked, and sorry, and try to understand—but, you see, they have not observed these things with their own eyes, and so . . .'

'I know what you mean,' Roger agreed. 'What

is imagined is not the same as what is seen.'

'No; and perhaps they will never quite comprehend just why we came here, and what we did. And yet—my father allowed me to do so. He could have prevented me, had he chosen.'

'He must be a remarkable man.'

'He is, indeed. You will like him very much, I believe.'

There was a companionable silence.

'What will you do with your fortune, my darling?'

'Well—I know that you will touch none of it—you have made that very clear!' Her eyes smiled into his; then she lowered her lids. 'However—it is possible, I believe, to provide a trust fund—' She blushed slightly, the lashes fanning out on her cheeks. 'For—for the children, Roger.'

He caught her up against him, and said with a laugh in his voice,

'I think that is a splendid idea, love!'

'And—perhaps you would not object, if—just now and then—I were to purchase a new gown?'

'Good God!' he exclaimed, conscience-stricken. 'What a churl you must think me! As if I should tell you what to do with your own property—! You may purchase a hundred gowns, if you choose!'

'Thank you! But I don't think I shall need a hundred gowns, or even fifty! However—I see no reason why we should not live in a pleasant house, with some of the elegancies of life. After all,' she added blithely, 'you will very soon be a Fellow of the Royal College, and one of London's most eminent physicians, and more than likely be knighted as well! We shall be obliged to keep up a style that is suited to your position, love!'

He burst out laughing, hugging her tightly. They rocked together like children in each other's arms.

With her face in his neck, she said indistinctly,

'Of course . . . there will still be money left—a great deal of it. And for that—I have a plan.'

'May I hear it?'

'Certainly you may. Indeed, you must, for I shall need you to help me and to advise me. I have not quite thought it out properly, yet . . . Grindle shall have a part in it, and Rachel too, I very much hope. And when I have worked out what is best to do, I shall tell you all about it . . .' She sighed, happily; her drowsy eyes strayed to the window. 'Roger! Do you know that it is almost dawn?'

'Yes, and you are hopelessly compromised,' he said promptly. 'You must marry me, Lady Eustacia. There is now no other course open to you.'

She gurgled deliciously.

'Indeed, sir, I am obliged! And both our families must see us married! Your father, and your mother; I want them to be there!'

A shade of doubt crossed Roger's face.

'I don't know whether my father . . . You see, my darling, he is going to disapprove of this marriage! It may seem odd to you; but he is a proud man, and set in his ways—'

She laid a finger on his lips, and sent him a roguish sidelong look sparkling through her lashes.

'Since I have met his son, I understand perfectly! When we return to England, you shall take me into Somerset, to visit your parents—I do so wish to know them, love! And also—you will want to see Gwen Willett, and her baby; a splendid boy, Roger—you will be delighted with him—'

'Yes, indeed; I am eager to see Danny's son.'

'Well! And whilst we are with your parents, I shall talk—just the two of us—with your mother. *She* will then persuade your father; between us we shall coax him around to giving his blessing! See if I am not right!'

'I am very sure you are. You will twine them both around your finger, just as you have already done with me . . . I love you, Tess Mainwaring!'

Her response to this was fervent and highly satisfactory. At last, a good deal dishevelled, she planted both palms against his chest and gasped,

'It is going to be the happiest wedding! Rachel, and Grindle, and our very truest friends—Oh! The most wonderful wedding that ever was, love—since the world began!'

CHAPTER
TWELVE

'SHOULD MISS Nightingale be sent for?'

'No. At the outset, Mrs Thiele forbade it. We do not care to disregard her expressed wishes.'

They were all there; nurses, surgeons, attendants. Some stood just within the door, others were waiting in the hall outside. Death was already in the room. The place seemed full of shadows, whispers, flickering white caps, the soft pad of feet. Distress was heavy in the air.

Tess's throat ached unspeakably; one of the other nurses wiped tears from her eyes. They had all seen so much death that it had become familiar, almost intimate; so commonplace that the mystery had long gone, and they had not realised that there could be so much sadness, a sorrow that was both bitter and futile, in so insignificant an event as a woman dying.

Grindle was standing quietly near the door. He saw the nurse who was weeping, and envied her because she could cry, while he must wait composed and expressionless in the grip of a misery that was personal and deep for the passing of a woman whom he scarcely knew.

Tess stood with her hand locked in Roger's.

Mrs Thiele stirred.

The movement was so slight as to be almost imperceptible, but the watchers grew still, and leaned closer, scarcely breathing—tyring to catch a murmured word.

Roger spoke without voice into Tess's ear.

'She may waken—for a moment—before the end.'

The senior nurse's eyelids flickered. Waveringly, by slow degrees, she swam up to the surface of her twilight world. Her half-opened lids reflected the pale ray of the bedside lamp, and the slight flame seemed to guide her; she looked at it, half-dreaming.

Then her eyes opened fully, to see them all there, about her.

Almost she smiled at them. Her mouth creased into tiny lines at the corners, seeing them anxious, weeping, grieving. She lingered for a moment on Tess, standing close at Roger's side. The nurse who was crying gave a little sob, and the tired eyes rested on her, and then slid past. She had comforted so many, eased so many, in the dark watches that they had all kept together, she and they . . . But now she could give them no more help. It was time, now, for her to rest.

She made a little gesture with her hand; it included them all. The body that scarcely lifted the covers settled into stillness; her eyes began to close.

Mary whispered, 'She is going . . .'

They were all startled by the calm clarity of the voice that came from the pale lips. Even in that moment, the tone was steady, and the echo of authority was in it still.

'I wish,' stated Mrs Thiele, faintly but definitely, 'to be buried here.'

With humble deference, Mr Crockford answered,

'I understand, ma'am. It shall be exactly as you wish.'

There was nothing more. They stood, waiting; the chaplain's lips moved in prayer.

She closed her eyes, with a last flutter of breath, and was gone so quietly that even those closest to the bed did not at first realise it.

It was spring again in the Crimea when the two young lovers came to the graveyard at Therapia for the last time.

'I don't even know—really—who she was,' Tess said sadly. 'Where did she come from? Had she been married? What did she think about, all those long hours when she was ill?' Her lip quivered; she leaned her head on his shoulder. 'I only know that she was a nurse; that's all. There's nothing else—'

'A nurse,' said Roger above her head, 'and a great lady.'

'Yes . . . a great lady. That is how I shall remember her.'

Their hands reached out, and clung.

A zephyr of a breeze blew through the graveyard, and the trees were already out in leaf. The grass was speckled with wild-flowers and the fragrance of new growth was in the air. Some solemn old cypress trees marched up the slope, and the shadows between them were like green cloisters shot through with bright gold. The fresh leaves twinkled under the April sun. Now and then, light and airy shadows travelled up and down the smooth slopes, as though wings were sweeping past in the sky, above the rows of wooden crosses. Tess and Roger had placed flowers on the mound at their feet; the pale bright blossoms rested lightly, delicately, on the new turf. The whole place had a warm and shimmering quietude, imparted by the brilliance of the light and the purity of the blue above them, like the under-surface of a dreamy and translucent sea.

Tess sighed, 'It is so beautiful here.' She made a gesture that embraced the plot before them, and the others that surrounded them in every direction. 'Roger . . . all this . . . Will it— happen again, do you think?'

He looked away over her head. His eyes held something distant—almost strange.

'Yes. It will happen again.'

She shuddered, and shrank against him. He put his arm about her.

'But—we'll go on, Tess . . . You and I.'

'Yes.' She nestled close within his arm. 'And—I shall know, love, that always—as each day ends—someone in pain, or fear, or sorrow, has been helped by you—by your strength, Roger . . .'

He gathered her up against him. Half to herself, she murmured,

'And for those who are crippled, or homeless—there will be a place. Cottages for families and widows, or a hospital . . . With your help, I shall manage.' She stopped suddenly, and looked up at him. 'Roger—we have talked about my plan, and I know you will help me—but, love, I have suddenly thought; I shall not, I am afraid, be a stay-at-home wife! Shall you mind very much?'

'Mind!' He said huskily. 'I am more likely to die of pride in you, my Tess!'

She gave a contented sigh.

'That is all right, then. There is so much to be done when we reach home! I must find the right property to purchase—not too far from London, but large and pleasant . . . There are so many, and I cannot help them all! But some, at least, will have comfort—and happiness, and peace.'

The sun had fallen towards the west, and the sky began to glow, radiantly and beneficently, like the promise of a ripening summer.

'Tess—we must go. The boat will be waiting.'

'To be home—so soon! I can scarcely believe it—'

Arm in arm, they began to walk away. At the edge of the graveyard, Tess asked, with a lingering look,

'Shall we ever come back, love?'

'We shall—one day. But now—'

She turned to him, and caught her breath.

'Yes—now—! England!'

They looked at each other. Grey eyes lit up, and leaped to blue. Their faces grew bright—began to glow. Handfasted, they turned together and began to hurry across the grass.

They quickened their steps, and her long legs matched his easy stride. His battered tunic swung free from square shoulders; her grey cloak blew out like a flag. The two heads, brown and gold, were lifted, eager, looking forwards, looking upwards.

Their figures dwindled and grew small under the sky. Beneath the colonnade of the tall old cypress pines, they passed from sight.

Perhaps there was music, around and far, or a muffled drum beating, or the throb of great wide ruffled wings—or perhaps it was only the blowing wind.

'England . . .'

The Norman chapel at Ribston Castle was lit with sun and candlelight and decked for a wedding.

In the gallery the choir sang softly. Great shining vases of white roses stood about, and there was trailing greenery, and white satin on the pews. The voices of the singers blended with the singing of birds in the garden outside the narrow windows. From these, it was possible to glimpse a sweep of ancient lawn that stretched in velvet green to the wooded slopes and down through the extensive and lovely grounds to the edge of the lake. The castle dreamed in the light of a June afternoon, and the walls, and the towers, and the heavy blossoming vines drowsed under the sun, while the lake was a blue mirror, shining back a bright reflection of the blue distances above.

Within the chapel, a handful of people were gathered, sitting quietly, occasionally exchanging a few words in low voices in the high carved pews towards the front of the nave.

Rachel and Grindle were seated side by side.

A becoming straw bonnet, pleated and lined with soft pink, was set on Rachel's glossy head. Her neat waist was bounded by a pink sash, and the white frills of her muslin dress spilled over on Grindle's knee. He leaned close to her, and whispered,

'If you don't mind me saying so, miss—you look a treat.'

She gave him an affectionate smile.

'Thank you. I return the compliment.'

Grindle was a living triumph of the power of spit and polish. Everything that could be made to gleam, gleamed; his hair was slicked flat with oil;

his new boots shone like glass.

He beamed, 'Never thought I'd find meself in a place like this—straight, I didn't!'

Rachel pressed his hand and turned her tranquil eyes towards the altar. She thought of the many weddings that had been witnessed there in the long centuries past; tall knights, and jewelled ladies with proud faces—almost, she could see their shadows, standing before those old stone steps to make their vows.

Many successive generations of Mainwarings had embellished, ornamented and enriched the stark grey stone walls and the oak pews that were black with age. The ceiling was sapphire blue, encrusted with golden stars, and every wall was hung with Venetian brocades, splendid and glowing in red and gold. A marvellous Florentine cloth, intricately embroidered, adorned the altar. Ornaments and lamps of baroque silver and gold shone and glimmered in niches and shadowy corners.

Grindle said in a breathy undertone, 'Ain't it a sight to see!'

Rachel smiled, and her eyes turned a little to consider the backs of the various persons seated in front of them.

The Countess of Cumnor and Lady Lucienne were nearest to the aisle; mother and daughter were sumptuously gowned in rich peacock blue and shimmering gold, respectively. They were certainly a magnificent pair, thought Rachel, and as kind as they were beautiful; Tess's mother had greeted her with the warmest affection; Lucy had accepted her instantly as a friend. Lucy's resemblance to her twin sister was quite remarkable, and yet Rachel did not really see how anyone could possibly confuse the two. Lady Lucy was startlingly lovely, and lively, and sweet; but, to Rachel, there was something in Tess's face which her sister lacked . . . a suggestion of thoughtfulness, perhaps; a touch of underlying gravity which added depth to her character. Lady Lucy turned a glowing countenance to catch some remark of her husband's; Rachel contemplated Lord Carseldine for a minute or two. He was very handsome, to be sure, only rather moody, by his looks—Lucy, however, did not seem to be in any awe of him.

Rachel turned her gaze a little more, and so came to the Viscount Mainwaring.

When Tess had presented her brother Justin, Rachel had been struck by the similarity of their features. Justin had his mother's clear green eyes, and his hair was auburn, but the likeness was arresting, all the same. His smile was also the most engaging that had ever caused an unwary female—with sense enough to know better—a sudden flutter of the heart. Tess had once told her, laughing, that if all the young ladies who yearned after her brother were laid end to end they would reach to John o' Groats . . . A vagrant sunbeam strayed in, and touched the back of the Viscount's head to copper. Oh! I can readily believe it, thought Rachel ruefully, and wrenched her eyes and her thoughts firmly in another direction.

Roger's parents were on the other side, in the front pew across from the Mainwarings. Mrs Verrall's silver-grey silk gown and her satin bonnet almost exactly matched the clear eyes that were so like her son's. Her gloved hands were folded in her lap, and her placid face composed; although every now and then she looked at her husband for a moment, as if to gain support from him. Roger's father, Rachel thought, had the same eagle profile as his son; his shoulders were a little bent, but he carried about him an air of solid pride and quiet strength, seated there in his good broadcloth suit, with his stout shoes planted foursquare on the stone flagged floor.

Roger stood alone, before the altar steps.

He stood still, and straight, and strong. In his breast pocket, Rachel knew, was a particular little silver ring, with a true lovers' knot on top. He had given it to Tess when first they had met; afterwards, when she had thought him lost, all through the long months of sadness and pain, she had kept it—hidden away, a secret treasure . . .

It had belonged to his mother. Now, it was to be Tess's wedding ring. She would have no other.

The music suddenly swelled to the ceiling. There was a stir at the door.

Tess came down the aisle on her father's arm.

Rachel was aware of gold hair glinting through a misty veil, the sheen of pearls, silk flounces going past the pews in a wave of whispering white; but then, Roger turned to his bride—and Rachel saw only their faces, and the joy in their eyes.

The space where they stood seemed bathed and enclosed in a pool of light that would go with them, and stay about them, so that they moved freely within it—whatever they might do, and wherever they might go.

'I, Eustacia, take thee, Roger . . .'